PRASH AND RAS

PRASH AND RAS

N.D. WILLIAMS

PEEPAL TREE

First published in Great Britain in 1997
Peepal Tree Press Ltd
17 King's Avenue
Leeds LS6 1QS
England

ISBN 1 900715 00 7

For John & Zulaika,

Eric King & Joe Pereira

and for Roderick E.
&
Carroll M.

Ever living
Ever faithful
Ever sure
Selassie I Rastafari

– Bob Marley ("Rastaman Vibration")

"Lord, I got to keep on moving
where I can't be found."

– Bob Marley ("Keep on Moving")

MY PLANET OF RAS

In August 1969 Mr & Mrs Hans Braun arrived on the island of Jamaica. The purpose of their visit was to determine the whereabouts of their daughter Kristal Marie Braun, a student who had left Germany one month before on a vacation trip to the island, and had not returned. Mr & Mrs Braun had received no communication from their daughter since the day they saw her off at the airport.

While on the island they sought the help of the police, the press and a Government Minister. A photograph of Kristal Marie Braun was published in the newspapers, and islanders were asked to get in touch with the authorities if they had any information.

Five days after their arrival a package was received by the editor of one of the island's newspapers. It contained a journal written by Kristal Marie Braun. It clearly established that Kristal Marie Braun had arrived on the island and had spent some time on the North Coast. The journal was examined by the police and by Mr & Mrs Braun, but it appeared to offer few clues to her whereabouts.

Two days later a man describing himself as a poet telephoned the police. He said he had met someone fitting the description of the missing Kristal Marie Braun, and that in the course of conversation he had learnt that Ms Braun had planned to attend a rock concert scheduled to take place in the state of New

*York, USA. It was his belief that she had indeed left the island
for the USA.*

*For days not much else was heard about the matter. There
was rumour and speculation that Kristal Marie Braun might
have been murdered.*

*Then a newspaper journalist reported speaking with mem-
bers of the Rastafari religious faith who claimed they knew of
her whereabouts. They said that the journal had in fact been
written and sent by Kristal Marie Braun; that she was alive and
in good spirits; and that she expressed no desire to meet or return with her parents.*

*A copy of the journal was secured by the poet, and with his
permission is partially reproduced below in translation for anyone still curious about what happened to Kristal Marie Braun
in August 1969.*

I

– As for my first impression, that critical first embrace of
the light, the ocean wind which the brochures promise would
be everywhere, sounds of native friendliness, the balm of the
tropics that takes away all the dull pounding aches we complain of in modern cities: *no pain here*, I thought, *at least for a
while.* And I thought: *it's going to be fine*, even as I stumbled
like a child down the aisle of the plane, the blood in my legs
running free again after hours in a cramped position.

Globules of fear from tiny pins of anxiety jabbing me here
and there; *but it's going to be just fine*, I thought. *No more pain.*

In fact, I was smiling, and for one simple reason: it's always
the way I prepare to face the *difference* outside: guards at any
border crossing, a stranger in a cafe who touches you and apolo-
gises, other situations of eye-shifting scrutiny and invitation.

At the door of the plane, I hesitated; I let the evening breeze gently garland my hair, put a smooch on my weary face.

You glimpse faraway blue water; you imagine there's a beach in that direction; white sand and blue water like the backyard of heaven rimming the entire island. The terminal building is a fragile, uncomplicated structure; there are people on the waving gallery, dark faces in simple clothes. You notice all this quickly; you want to rush off the plane, skip across those procedural stones, link hands and dance right away.

I knew I'd made the right choice after all, coming to this small place; not going off like an American hippie to India in search of some holy grail; not wandering down some dark alley, inviting death by happenstance.

What is the purpose of your visit, they like to ask.

People go to small countries because *I want to get away; I need a vacation; it's so exotic, all those smiling friendly faces, you feel like royalty for a week*. For me this small place, this speck on the map, was at the other end of everything I had always known, at the push of a button, on the edge of a chip; many thousands of miles, many hours away from your crib, your parents' home, their waiting plot, our heaven or hell.

An island unlike any you've heard or read about, the girl at travel agency said, puzzled, staring.

Though why would you want to go there, you heard her thinking, even as she checked her schedules and talked about connections. She couldn't see my squirrelly eyes dead behind dark glasses, and in any case couldn't understand the impulse to take oneself away, like a coal miner's woman who has known only his lung-clogging dust all her life.

Well, one could use a vacation – in any faraway place that is not too familiar, like Timbuktu. Clean air, blue skies.

Which made the girl at the travel agency smile: islands were, indeed, useful and usable; and in any case there was one hour left before a lunch date with her boyfriend.

The only small place I knew in my city was the bathroom; it was there that they found me, rushed me to hospital, pumped out my stomach, handed me over to my mother and father for recuperative attention.

You don't need a vacation, my mother said. *Everything you need is here. You are all we have.* My father bit his lips and said nothing.

There would be no one on the island who resembled Klaus. No one who could possibly speak like him, with his sullen ideological passion; no one to spread my legs like butterfly wings; and when I fluttered, screaming yes and no, no one would say to me, "Christ, you're a pathetic creature! Your masochism bores me to tears".

The smallest place, then, next to the grave, where something smelling of stillborn love could be laid to rest; an island, with white beaches and palm trees, or so the girl imagined, knowing only good restaurants in the city and her boyfriend's weekend lust; and a friendly Immigration clerk who would be satisfied with only a driver's licence, a credit card, your willingness to lie on your back and be massaged by clear blue waters; a pretty island girl steering me toward a table where complimentary rum punch was waiting; and outside a smiling porter with a red cap and a round face signalling for a taxi.

Everything you need is accessible.

Well, yes, everything was. But the sun was going down and though there were many days ahead when the same sun would give a similar performance I wanted to watch this, my first tropical sunset, like my first love, moving swiftly to some consummation behind that spread of hills.

So I found a bench outside and arranged myself like a guest watching a parade of fading light.

The sun left a pinkish glow on the hills; people moved about in a languid, dreaming way. I was ready to run or jump or fly.

I wasn't sure what my next step would be, though there were round-faced porters signalling taxis that would take you to rooms at reasonable rates and a meal and a map of the island. I was happy simply to be here.

It wasn't going to be that easy; I imagined *the difference* would come over me like a gentle drizzle that wets but means no harm, leaving you slightly amnesiac.

Well, the sunset vanished quickly; all at once it was dark, not a creepy threatening dark, just that absence of points of light that help you locate your fear: all at once I felt Klaus slipping out of memory the way his penis softened and slipped away when he was finished; I shivered a little for the evening breeze was lovely but unusually cool on my skin; it was like that, too, whenever he was finished: an abrupt getting out of bed to put on his underwear, making me reach for the sheets to cover my nakedness, to simulate the warmth of his arms around me, needing warmth right at that point, not my underwear; at which moment the airport began to feel deserted, as if one big plane had flown in, released its burden, and taken off, and that was all for now, until the next incoming day; all of which needs to be said, for it was in this state, shivering and alone, that I had touched down on the Planet of Ras.

He might have been standing in front of me like a century-old tree watching my face buried in a pillow of forgetting; he might have said the same words several times before they finally penetrated:

"Hail, in the name of the conquering Lion of the Tribe of Judah."

"Hello," I said softly, smiling.

I remember staring at his face, at the high cheek bones, the pouch of his hat, curling strands of the beard he kept twisting with his fingers; a diminutive man, with a lion tamer's voice; the empty parking lot behind him, and the airport building which seemed locked up for the night, its entrances and exits vacant, its operations suspended so that everyone could get back to contemplating palm trees and sunsets.

"Stranger to our shores?" he asked.

"Yes."

"We have a little proposition."

"And who are we?" I asked, enjoying this quick mystifying courtship.

"Come," he said, "meet the bredren. The Twelve Tribes of Israel."

SELASSIE: READER, HEALER WITH HERBS
IKAEL: ARTIST-PAINTER
KILMANJARO: MASTER DRUMMER

"Light up a spliff for the visitor from *fareign*," Selassie said, a little imperiously. He had led me across the car park to a solitary vehicle against which two of his friends lounged like limousine chauffeurs; they offered greetings; they squatted and set about making a marijuana cigarette, while Selassie, leaning on a polished walking stick, said to me:

"You know of *the herb*? You know of what people here refer to, criminally, as *ganja*, but what I man know personally to be *the healing of the nations*?"

I told him I had heard about marijuana but had to confess I'd never tried it.

"Well, right now, you will taste the goodness thereof. You

come from *fareign*. The journey inland is long and hard. Burning herb in the temple give strength to the spirit."

The goodness thereof! From fareign!

And "the journey inland" turned out to be part of the proposition; he would take me in his car all the way to the North Coast, which is where the tourists go, if I were willing to pay for the petrol, the fuel tank, like their pockets, at the moment empty.

Such instant partnership! There was a gentle feeling about them, an ancient ease; I was charmed by their lean bearded angular hardened looks, the Bible-based language of their planet.

I looked around me: a lingering sense that awhile ago a plane had landed, a door had opened, I had stepped out, the glass doors of that building were the last mirrors of my blue eyes and shoulder-length blond hair, knapsack, khaki shorts; and now I was invited to share in a ritual eating of *the herb* by the Ras, who squatted on haunches, and passed the cigarette from lip to hand to lip, an elegance in the wrist, until it came to me, sitting like a happy girl guide around a campfire, coughing a little at my turn, watching the strange intensity with which each man sucked, cheeks hollowed, on that carrot of a cigarette, my turn again, a light-headed feeling of wellbeing, lights in the distance, no longer an island, an unknown planet, and the first men to step out of memory capsules, their knees almost touching chins, their bodies forked as if slowly thawing out from some cramped spaceship-hold, the circling herb, my turn again, and Selassie declaring:

"Time to make a move. Draw away one last time. Long journey inland through the night over the hills. The herb come like a lifeline, holding you, so the spirit don't cut away, send you spinning weightless back where you come from."

This is how the journey inland began.

What came before – from the moment the girl handed me
the airline ticket and wished me a pleasant trip, to the puzzled
look on the face of the red capped attendant whose offer to find
a taxi I'd refused – all preparation, mere doorways you pass
through to this: the last draw on the cigarette, the swelling har-
monies of peace in my head, the aroma of the herb like incense
dispelling all evil forces on this island planet, turning our separate obsessions toward one salvation: the hand passing the herb
in golden circle.

So we're rattling along a stretch of roadway, traffic coming
the other way, passing in a *swoosh*, Kilmanjaro at the controls
of the car. He hunches over the wheel; when he changes gears
the engine howls, his feet shift between pedals ecstatically,
going faster and faster, the car shaking as he punishes it into
higher speed, then howling when we're forced to slow, so that
at times I fear the doors would rip away, the wind force sucking us out.

Selassie senses my anxiety and tells Kilmanjaro to *main-
tain a balance.*

"Always the same with him," he explains ruefully, "once
him get behind a wheel, twin demons pulling him both ways."

"Hear him!" Kilmanjaro retorts. "Like the Governor in the
back seat driving to Parliament."

Ikael is sitting in the front seat, his face stuck out the window as if inviting and enjoying the lash of the wind. I want to
ask him to shut the window. The wind keeps blowing my hair
all over my face.

Stretches of empty road, lamp posts like dutiful centurions
lighting our way, the dark hump of the hills, the sea, the smell
of rotting fish.

And then the headlights of something approaching, perhaps
a delivery truck (if the road were an autobahn), bearing down
on us across the dividing line like some huge machine craving

blood and steel and broken bones. Kilmanjaro sees it, but is
unwilling to give way until the very last moment, when with my
eyes closed, we seem to pass through the roaring bowels of the
truck, the air churning up around us, and then through the anus
in a *whoosh*.

"*Demon of self-destruction!*" Ikael shouts. "You going to kill
us, Rasta?" He sounds more quizzical than angry.

Selassie switches on a transistor radio nestling in his lap;
he pulls the antennae out as far as it goes; he fiddles with the
tuning knob, racing through frequencies spewing voices, static,
music; he gives up suddenly in disgust.

"Babylon's babel," he says to me, shaking his head wearily; then he slips in a cassette.

A voice wails, a guitar scratches the air, drums dig up graves
of the past; at high volume, they compete with the car's gears
and the wind.

I want to ask Selassie to switch it off; his fingers rub the
shiny chrome of the antennae; I lean back instead; I close my
eyes; I bite my lips as words of remonstration rise in my throat;
I swallow the words, not wishing after all to risk discord; I keep
my eyes closed, and recall as a child watching a fire-eater in a
circus and wondering how he did it, how with one gulp he ate
red flame.

At some point we left the highway which on the island is
any empty stretch of road inducing speed and collision; entering a town, joining a flow of traffic, billboards with eyes that
follow yours, neon, shops, people at bus stops, laughing faces;
naturally you want to stop the car, step up to that coconut ven-
dor, tilt your head back and drink, mingle and marvel, taste
more of those lilting accents.

But the windows of the car were now wound up tight as if
the air outside were fetid or poisoned with invisible particles
of death-hastening dust.

"Babylon's refuse, after the sunset of Empire," Selassie explained, like some disgruntled tourist guide wishing to extinguish any flame of excitement.

I made an effort not to lean forward, to sit back and take in the island with something resembling their reserve, their disavowal of responsibility for what moved outside: a bazaar of coming and going to be viewed from behind our grime-streaked windows; a randomness and disarray through which we, destined for the North Coast, were merely passing.

Then Kilmanjaro made a turn into Empire Boulevard, an improbable piece of roadway, an experiment in modern improvement, commonplace in London or Frankfurt, you might think; drenched in sodium light, curving cleanly; miniature trees with solid trunks, evenly spaced along the sidewalk; an aberration of sorts, kept free of coconut vendors, condemned to live up to its designer's vision of the island's future.

"Roadway to the Prime Minister's residence," Selassie whispered; then he caught his breath as Kilmanjaro, who had been driving with a chauffeur's deference to the road designer's dream, suddenly hit the brakes.

There was someone walking in the middle of the road: a black figure, a tall, naked man, possessor of the empty night, bare buttocks, sagging knees, arms outstretched as if in surrender or jubilant embrace.

Kilmanjaro slowed, then decided to overtake cautiously to his right; he chose not to sound his horn; something about the black figure, its profile deranged in the light, made him untouchable, to be skirted at a harmless distance.

As we passed we all felt compelled to look back; the man's head was lowered in weariness or meditation; a mass of hair, thick as lianas, obscured his face; his long limp sex swung in front of him like a metronome. It was all I could do to conceal my embarrassment. My fascination. I might not have stared like that if it were at all possible to see his face.

"An ex-Minister of Home Affairs?" Kilmanjaro smirked, picking up speed again.

"An apparition," Selassie said to me. "Pretend you never see it."

"No, Rasta," Ikael declared. "We all did see it. A naked black man walking alone on Empire Boulevard. No apparition, that. Some kind of stark metaphor."

"Him is a painter," Selassie said, referring to Ikael, and trying to take the seriousness out of the air. "Him like to worry the air, scratching for the reality beneath reality. Be patient with him."

"Cho, wait till you see my next painting," Ikael said folding his arms.

"So tell us what *you* see, daughter," Kilmanjaro said, twisting his head to look at me, catching me unawares. I laughed, a little confused, trying to shake the question off before it crawled like an insect under my shirt.

I said, "Well, what did I see? I saw: a man on his way to the showers!"

There was a moment of silence, the balloon swelling larger with air, then everyone almost simultaneously burst out laughing. I laughed too, surprised and happy to have touched them that way. Then we all fell silent, until Ikael, whose head must have been spinning with images for his next painting, said:

"Poor Israelite!"

A remark that didn't explode with meaning until much later.

We began a spine-jolting zigzag along a narrow road; it was more like a footpath, barely wide enough to accommodate the car; it was severely cratered and littered with thrown-away objects waiting in the dark to stab at our tyres.

A horrible odour thick as fog swept inside the car, wrapping itself around my head. It slipped inside me and sank to the bottom of my stomach. Soon I felt the first bubbles of nausea.

A shout from Ikael alerted Kilmanjaro. Near the side of the road lay the bloated corpse of a dead animal, its legs stiff and upright. Kilmanjaro saw it, worked furiously at the wheel, swerved, but not in time. I felt something squelch under the tyres and instantly I wanted to be sick.

We sideswiped a steel drum to the left. Selassie had simply braced himself; nothing he could do; he grinned; more of the stench poured in, oozing down my stomach.

"I think we ran over that dead animal," I said, as if the incident had to be noted.

We jolted into a pothole and Kilmanjaro swore an apology for not seeing it in time. The headlights were bright on sagging zinc fences, leaning gateways, shacks, thick vegetation, a scrawny dog sniffing at garbage. And we had run over a dead animal; we were carrying its coiled innards and stench on our tyres.

When abruptly we stopped, the motor still running, I was wondering why we had to, here of all places.

"Soon come," Ikael said, getting out and vanishing through a hole in the zinc fence.

Kilmanjaro got out too; he pulled up the handbrake, made a little theatre as he stretched his limbs, then he walked behind the car; with his back toward us, legs apart, one hand rather showily akimbo, he released his bladder, his urine crashing against the fence.

The nausea surged, fell back, surged again. I opened the door and waited. I felt its slushy passage up and then along the wall of my tongue. I retched violently. I was surprised at the sound of my retching, an awful animal sound. I vomited again, spitting out the aftertaste; then I shut the door and felt like crying.

Selassie pulled at my sleeve; he was offering the herb.

"Will put you all right. Take you far away from here," he said. His smile, the twirls in his beard, the way his head inclined brought back that curious kindness with which he had greeted me at the airport. I pulled at the herb and began to feel better.

Once we were at ease again, he led me farther away from that place by offering a slice of personal history. It was the year 1938 – "at the crucial tilt of the historical axis" – when Mussolini dared to invade the sacred land of Ethiopia, and the hands of Europe were once more stained with the blood of the lamb. It was a time when Emperor Haile Selassie repelled the forces of darkness, hurling back those armies of cropped hair obsession, and throwing in reverse the fortunes of the whole of Europe. In that year, he said, his mother gave birth to her only son...

"Roadblock! Babylon out tonight. Wickedness at large."

There was resentment but little surprise in Selassie's voice; a weary resentment at the jeep parked across the roadway, at the police officer brandishing a rifle and signalling us to stop. Kilmanjaro and Ikael exchanged words in low syllables; they seemed to be calculating their chances of making a run for it, measuring the gap between the front end of the Police Jeep and the roadside ditch.

There were other men in uniforms, with bony faces and holstered pistols, waiting; the man with the rifle waved his hands vigorously, then stiffened as if to warn us he meant business; his body was thin; it didn't wear authority too well; he held the rifle with unaccustomed hands; no soldier, he was a man with a gun who wanted us to stop or else he'd fire his gun. He frightened me; the others in the car, still talking in a meas-

ured drawl, were seeing beyond him to the stage-set of una-
voidable confrontation.

"Switch off the headlights before that one start shooting,"
Selassie advised. "Step out the car, go talk to them, before them
mash up everything."

Kilmanjaro got out and approached the vehicle. From the
darkness of our car we watched.

Unable to hear what was being said we had to interpret the
language of gesture: Kilmanjaro's languid gait, all frailty and
innocence; the man with the rifle, now casual in command
awaiting the next move; another officer, bulky, chest swollen
inside the authority of his uniform.

Then Kilmanjaro raised his hands, allowing himself to be
patted in what seemed a search for weapons; they wanted to
search his pockets; he pulled back and must have protested
that intrusion. The man with the rifle hit him in the ribs; his
body went limp absorbing the blow, but he kept his feet.

A sigh slipped from Selassie; he was watching intently from
the back seat, making no move; I turned to him, baffled and
frightened; he had offered an explanation for everything so far;
I needed to understand this violence quickly.

Then it was Ikael's turn to lose patience; he growled as he
got out and approached the jeep. He removed his hat, releasing a shower of long hair (dreadlocks) down his shoulders; he
looked like an ancient warrior; he walked like a gleaming angry sword.

Now we could hear voices. Ikael's was high-pitched and
righteous with protest. The officers were momentarily taken
aback, then they moved to confront this new presence; grab-
bing at Ikael's locks, his arms, wrestling with him, then dragging him behind the headlights.

A brief chilling silence; my body felt suddenly cold. Whatever happened, I didn't want to be hit by that rifle; I didn't want to be touched by those hands.

We heard the first scream, a long howl, as of a man struck in the groin; then voices firing at will, spilling emotions like blood.

Another howl, another soaring streamer of pain, cut short this time by curses. The man must have swung his rifle butt again, trying for clean powerful blows to the body's tender core; Kilmanjaro and Ikael must have struggled to free their arms, screaming the purest innocence and rage.

"Persecution fall upon the meek like rain," Selassie declared, shifting his bottom. "All 'cause them won't conform to false images, cut their locks and worship false creeds. The meek wouldn't inherit this earth," he said.

"What are we going to do?" I asked.

"Colonysation thrown in reverse. Maybe you can rescue this situation," Selassie said.

I looked at him open-mouthed, even as the rifle butt raised huge bruises on our hearts. What could *I* possibly do out there to stop this?

"*White authority! Coldstream guards! Khaki drill and stiff-hand salute!...* Those idiots inflicting pain on the bredren will melt in the heat of white authority. Leftover from colonial days... But watch here now, you could play any role, majesty or whore, and put a stop to this foolishness; you could walk on that stage right now, and change their capacity for cruelty and casualty."

Muffled cries of pain clawed at the air. There was no time for elaboration or script.

Dimly I understood what I had to do, so assuming Selassie was right about personas in black/white dramas, ghosts of the past, I stepped out, the ground under my feet unfamiliar, walked up to the jeep; and *Stop this, what are you doing? These*

*men are with me. We're on our way to the North Coast. My hus-
band is the Manager of the Paradise Hotel. You have no right
doing this. We know the Chief of Police*, and other noises of
outrage that caught everyone nakedly unawares, gave them no
time to interrupt my flow of authority... and while Ikael and
Kilmanjaro hurried back to the car, a change of tact, a touch of
sympathy for the officer in charge, *I know the difficult job you
have to do*, which elicited an embarrassed smile, a mumbled
apology, while we climbed back into the vehicle, and away we
drove once more into the night, nursing our wounds with the
laughter that salves bruised dignity, the herb that heals all
time-gapped wounds...

Then the car starts climbing; twisting and turning around
innumerable bends, and climbing. Fatigue sits on my eyelids
like a stone; I fight to stay awake.

Kilmanjaro drives close to the mountain face; he's wary of
the sheer drop on our right. Besides, vehicles would occasionally and without warning spring out of the dark upon us with
roaring blinding beams. By some miracle we pass each other,
lucky not to collide.

Higher and higher into some colder region.

To locate and appease my fear I imagine a castle perched
on the mountain top. This is our destination. I see an old couple – my mother and father – standing at the gates, looking out
for us; smiling, they rush our fatigued bodies inside as soon as
we arrive, instructing the servants at this late hour to prepare
food, drink, warm beds...

Higher and higher, until we start coming down the other
side, still snaking around bends, staying close to the mountain
face; through a sleepy town, its marketplace deserted, the clock
at the roundabout unlit; past dwellings, shuttered shops, stray
dogs, a vagrant singing.

In the car a weary, contemplative silence. Ikael would point to a road sign; Kilmanjaro farts; Selassie, drawn back to the transistor, would fiddle with the tuning knob.

Are we nearly there? I wonder.

"Almost reach."

"I man feel it long time back. Strange how before you even turn the last bend you know you near the place. Your heartbeat change rhythm, your hair ends stand up, the wind like it rolling in anguish 'cross the sky."

"Ever feel to stop?"

"No, Rasta. I man can mesh with the wailing, but this is just a short-cut. I man just passing through."

"Coming up to the bridge."

"Irie!"

"Watch the curve, don't run off the road. Stay in first, and keep to your left."

I'm looking outside but there is no coastline.

"Where are we?" I ask. "How much longer to the North Coast?"

"*Village of Unending Sorrow*. Keep your eyes open," Selassie says to me.

I rub my arms for the air has turned chilly all of a sudden. We cross the bridge; its loose planks rumble under the wheels like thunder; then it starts to rain. There is no warning drizzle; a chill in the air, the crossing of a bridge, then heavenly downpour.

It slows our progress, almost by design; the road is now a river of running water reducing us to a crawl. The windshield wipers swish uselessly; Kilmanjaro clears vapour from the windows with a rag; we must now feel our way forward.

The houses are blurred and huddled, battened down, absorbing the drenching force. Coconut trees sway in barren agony; an interminable downpour that might have begun centuries ago. On an impulse Selassie winds down the window; the rain pelts in: wild cold drops of water spattering our faces, seeming to cling there.

I look at Selassie, bewildered; he makes no move to close the window. As I search for tissue I feel the rain moving on my face, slowly, forging the tiniest rivulet on my cheek, my nose, my arms; water moving like tears slipping away from the piti-ful hold of the eye. As more of the rain pelts in (raising mild groans from Kilmanjaro who nevertheless concentrates on driv-ing) dampening our clothes, as I struggle to wipe it away, I see the first faces; I hear many voices, singing or weeping, in dis-traught chorus.

They seem to sail past us, those faces, like human wreck-age, abandoned by some heartless captain and crew; at the same time they seem rooted like centuries-old trees; hands like gnarled branches reached out to us, waving or begging, plead-ing or praying; hands holding babies, with bald heads, bulging eyes, – "Tourist bus don't pass this way." – soaked faces of women, children, old men, more women – "Same way them used to line colonial routes to wave at visiting royalty." – voices calling after us: half-wail, half-summons; distinctly human cries over and above the whipping rainstorm, singing or weep-ing, the rain coming in, mingling with my tears, Selassie's tears – "Been like this, raining day and night, from I was a boy, from you were a girl, from every man's first childhood." My body is damp with pity and incomprehension. I wipe my eyes, but in-side other voices, singing or weeping, hang like thin yellowed leaves from branches on my heart.

You remember always your first morning anywhere, in a new country or a hotel, a friend's apartment: waking up in an unfa-miliar room whose walls do not reflect your preferences, the rent you pay, other fragrances of your occupancy.

I was lying on a mattress on the floor of a room. Someone had covered me with a blanket, a hand of kindness, and so I felt I was in no particular danger.

I lifted my head and in a detached puzzled way made a swift inventory of the room: several drums, a broom, shirts on wire hangers on nails, paintings stacked untidily against one wall, *my knapsack.*

The door to my room opened and like a magic genie Kilmanjaro bounced in, scaring me a little, for I'd never seen him before in broad daylight: a short, muscular man, in dreadlocks, one tooth missing; I wouldn't have recognised him had he not said, "At last, you surface from the deep. Come quickly, observe the glory of Jah in the morning."

The North Coast! We were on our way to the North Coast. We must have arrived during the night!

Kilmanjaro picked up one of the drums and was hurrying to the door. "If you don't make a move," he said, "you miss the miracle of Creation."

I didn't want to miss anything, considering that most everything so far – coming up to me now, like lost luggage, from the deep – had been just short of otherworldly; but my body, aching slightly from so torturous a passage, wanted time to adjust to the new atmosphere. I hesitated.

Kilmanjaro came back in with a freshly-folded *spliff*; I took it from his hand, feeling the glow of kindness in his smiling bearded face. I lay back; I smoked.

I looked outside at the sky framed by the room's single window; I had never done this before: lain on my back on a bare floor, feeling secure within bare wall and shelter, gazing at the sky as through the porthole of a spacecraft; never felt before such complete freedom from the many earthly fetishes you wake up to.

What made it more startling and unforgettable was the odour of limes from a tree outside my window that percolated through the morning.

Kilmanjaro's drumming now sounded like an urgent summons to throw off the blanket, for there was spectacle to be witnessed – *the miracle of creation*: so much obscure high drama promised in those words. I hurried to the door.

I stepped out into the gentle folds of distant hills wrapped in vaporous mist, over which the sun was climbing. Looking down, you saw a lush green valley; beyond that, grey surface of the sea, corrugated into stillness. Our house was perched on a hillside; it looked frail, made out of rudimentary materials; not so much a house, as an elaborate shelter erected by many bare hands from bamboo, galvanised sheets, coconut palms; and behind it, junglelike vegetation and trees from which the sound of birds was like a family blissfully at breakfast. I saw the bredren:

Kilmanjaro: in a procreative crouch, the drum gripped between his thighs, his hands like slapping blades; the drum was pointed towards the rising palace of the sun, and each rhythmic slap, mixing with particles of light, was like a million human feet ascending a stairway of ecstasy that stretched up from the goat skin to the sky.

Selassie: standing on the ledge of the hill, his body-builder's chest puffed like a peacock, his head thrown back, his squinting eyes surveying his kingdom of the infinite.

Ikael: tall and lean, face dark as coal, dancing with the weightless motion of an astronaut; his toes barely touch the ground, his legs lift off; his hands and his locks multiply; he is a laughing spider man, whirling gravity-free.

"Hail up!" Selassie shouts to me, waving me to join him. "I man thought you would sleep forever. Welcome to our window

to the universe. The planetarium, you might call it. But I man
see it differently."

"What a marvellous view," I said.

"More than a *view*, daughter. And in time you might marvel
at the many things you see. *Selassie I Rastafari!*"

He shouted those last words with defiance and praise and
wild jubilation. Such an arrangement of syllables and sibilants
I had not heard before.

"Call to the sea and sky. Fill up your lungs; empty your soul
of dead matter, dead habit. You stand before the miracle of
creation. You watching a process that began millions of years
before. Call to the sea and sky. Give thanks to the miracle of
your creation. *Selassie I Rastafari*."

"Selassie I Rastafari," I said laughing.

"No, daughter! Call like a child just born; scream like the
mother pushing that child; shout like a midwife giving comfort
to that miracle."

"Selassie-i-ras-tafari!" I cried.

"*Irie!*" he said, gently, approvingly.

II

So here we were, after a night that was like a mule's kick to
the imagination; and then a morning when it seemed as if a
ceremonial hand had raised the curtains over the universe to
reveal, for my astonishment or initiation, land sea and sky, sun
and later stars, vegetation and fruit – God's plenty or the miracle of creation.

It was the North Coast. I didn't know exactly where we were,
and for a while I had no wish to locate myself beyond the in-
stinctive trust, the herbal bond that joined me in spirit to the Ras.

Soon we settled into some kind of routine, our separate functions or dreaming occupations.

Kilmanjaro went off every morning to farm the land, planting herbs and vegetables that spared us journeys down the hill to local supermarkets. Ikael worked most of the day on his paintings, like an archaeologist knee-deep in the diggings of his private obsessions; Selassie, when he wasn't cooking up his *itals*, sat outside under a billion-leaf tree reading the Bible; often he paused to gaze lazily at grass or stone, or a hairy-legged insect journeying across the ridges of a leaf.

As evening fell, as twilight threw an orange shawl of serenity over sea and land, we would pull ourselves away from separate preoccupations, light up *spliffs* and share in prolonged silences or the most exhilarating conversations.

All of which left me with choices: attaching myself to any one activity or individual: (a) Selassie brooding over the Book of Revelation; (b) Kilmanjaro climbing the coconut trees like a frog, then pulling down coconuts that crashed to the ground like a revolution; (c) learning to use the cutlass without chopping off my foot.

I chose instead to swing gently in the hammock. I liked the curve of the hammock. I would lie there, drawing on a *spliff*, swinging gently, until my skin began to tingle, my body's pores opening to release beads of perspiration; for me this was an unparalleled sensation, one thousand times better than suntanning on any summery beach.

There were no intruders, no visitors, except a boy named Phanso who came at intervals, carrying a basket of cakes and fruit and home cookings prepared by his mother, which he exchanged for all the limes he could find under the lime tree.

Soon, after about a week (though you couldn't really tell one day from the next, Saturday night from Sunday morning) despite the heart-swelling view from the hill, our evenings in herbal haze, I became infected with a curious restlessness: a burning need simply to place a pin or a marker on some men-

tal map, telling yourself, you are *here*, and measuring in quick-
ened heartbeats the distance between that hereness and your
last memory post.

I would stare after the boy Phanso, making his way down
the hill along a dirt track, and wonder: where did he live? did
he have brothers and sisters? how did his mother bake those
corncakes?

Now and then, under the unfailingly blue sky, across the
sea's crinkled foil, you noticed the white speck of a yacht, you
heard the whine of a low-flying jet.

Something else too: call it an unconscious wish, to reach
back, to send a postcard to loved ones whose ageing eyes asked
worryingly, as they waved goodbye, *isn't it a bit risky, her going off alone to, where is this island?* all of which meant locat-
ing a post office, and then a shop with warning bells on its door,
a newspaper rack, other people out strolling...

One afternoon, slipping out from under the anywhereness
of the herb, I started down the track, intending merely to get to
the bottom of the hill, find a road and a road sign; intending no
more than to satisfy some need to make quick comparisons,
then hurry back.

There was first the rare sensation of stones and gravel under my bare feet, which turned my walk into an exploration of
territory and terrain. What had I been missing, I wondered,
after all these years of carpets, swept sidewalks and shoe
stores? This: the bruising love touch of bare earth, the washing
off of dry mud at the end of any journey, the massage of weary
feet by loving hands.

At the bottom of the hill, the road welcomed you with indifference and charm, going one way round a bend, going the other
then dipping out of sight. You long to make contact with some
indigenous other: a shirtless villager on a horse drawn cart, a

leathery old man in baggy pants driving before him an unruly family of sheep.

A grassy verge. An anyplace road, which nevertheless invited you like a lover to explore, discover new terrors or delights. I turned left and started walking.

I walked. I picked a random flower.

I heard a car coming up behind me just as I thought of crossing the road, and though it was safe to cross I chose to wait.

It was cadillac-sized, spacious, running sleek and silent, with the roof down. As it swept past I caught a glimpse of a peak-capped chauffeur, and then three bulbous pink faces wearing dark glasses, crammed in the back seat, wedged together like enormous stuffed dolls. Judging from their faces upturned to the sky, the distinct laid-back pleasure of those heads, they looked like human sponges soaking up as much of the sun as their vacation time allowed.

When it was time to turn back, despite the temptation to explore further, despite the real disappointment at not meeting anyone, a beach came into view. It was near enough for a rash detour, a quick trample through some underbrush, the yielding hot sand, the sky-reflecting water.

But off to the right, quite suddenly, a speedboat: its bow slicing and slapping the water: tourists having fun: the girl's hair streaming in the wind, the man displaying what must have impressed the girl as a beautiful bronzed body; his hands masterfully controlling the wheel; the bow lifting and plunging, sending up random spray that speckled their faces, salted their intimacy.

Then they were out of sight, leaving in their wake the emptiness of the ocean, whose churned surface seemed to sigh, to swell in passionate adaptations, then settle back into that vast patience you recognise after speedboats like Klaus have quite finished.

When eventually I came back up the hill Selassie was sitting under the tree, folding a spliff, trying to appear nonchalant, though I couldn't help feeling he was displeased about something.

"So what you discover down there?" he asked. His tone was flat; the question had a neutral ring, but I could tell he was piqued.

"Well," I said tentatively, "I saw an old pirate ship at anchor, and sailors cavorting on the beach with island women."

He didn't take that as I'd intended. It wasn't enough to close the gap between us.

"I saw the car that brought us here from the airport," I said.

Which was true. It lay abandoned in a ditch at the bottom of the hill, stripped of its tires; attacked by scavengers of metal, it seemed; barely recognisable as a vehicle whose shiny chrome once gave pride of ownership to someone; a spent hulk, whose brown rust was quietly returning to the earth, which in a way that was hard to explain made it so much more magnificent an object.

I sat beside him; he offered me the *spliff*; it seemed a gesture of forgiveness, whatever my indiscretion, my barely pardonable lapse.

"Something else," I said, after my first draw. "I met someone. An elderly woman, alone on the beach, buried up to her shoulders in the sand. I mean, all you saw was her head and arms in the sand under an open parasol; she was staring out to sea; her eyes were reddened from too much sun or sadness; so I said to her, What's the matter? Why do you chose to live like this? She barely looked at me, tilted her head as if looking down her nose; then she said, *Do you see what I see?* I looked out to sea; there was nothing there. *There's always something out there, on the horizon line or in the bush; always something thrashing about like a hog or rhinoceros.* I couldn't understand what she meant. *Sigh no more, dear, sigh no more, nightfall*

like a guillotine, "off with their clothes", sunrise a gorgeous
cock, "off with its head"; Oh please don't look at me like that,
you see, my husband and I should have returned after, you
know, all the foolish flag lowering, but he could never get
enough, never enough, rumpitty tump, rumpitty tump, you
know, rumpussy, rumpus, rump, rum. I rue the day we ever set
foot on this fornicating isle, do you see what I see? All gone; I
still have these terrible migraines, would you pass me those sun-
glasses, there's a good girl? I put her sunglasses on her face
and walked away, looking over my shoulders at her head, missing its torso of the old days; a coconut shell, all straggly hair
and parched skin, buried in the sand, waiting for the sea to
come rolling in, take it bobbing across the ocean. I left her there
and came home."

Selassie passed the *spliff*; he stretched out his legs and
sighed; his face was wrinkled with wonder; I could tell he was
pleased with what I'd just said, as if it were a stick of narrative
he himself had snapped from some century-old tree and had
thrown out for me to fetch.

I followed his gaze over the emptiness of the ocean, beyond
the horizon's rim, where at any moment, if you shared his intensity, it seemed you might witness something truly amazing.

I felt a need to talk some more, to make some idle comment
on the planet's smooth surfaces, on leaf or rock, surfaces wiped
clean by the sunlight's rag.

But something said, *Hush! Not a word! Look! What do you*
see? I gazed; I drew on the *spliff*; I had the feeling that the island would last forever, even as it was passing away, coming to
an end, like suffering and pain, memory and cold long nights.

"On vacation! I man know that well. Landlord, landowners
tell I & I vacate here, vacate there. Bredren deal with that all
the while – No Vacancy inside man's kingdom!"

"I don't think I've ever heard of Frobenius."

"Well, right now, at this midnight hour in human history, is like the tide turning home. The lost child reclaiming the Mother, scattered pieces rejoining the whole of Africa."

"Is not so it go. I man waiting for the flash, when Babylon crash."

"What is he talking about?"

"Him mean *the big mushroom*. The second dropping!"

"Then we invent it all over again, worlds within world, all over again!"

"I man have an idea for a painting. A new direction for I & I."

"You mean, *new distraction!* You're nothing but a blocked artist, dauber-man."

"New direction. I man call it *Ethiopian Memories*."

"Islands are loose women who never knew their fathers."

"Was pain coming through the middle passage. I man carry the agony of I forefathers, clear echoes in I bones. Pain is the passage back, through redemption, to new beginnings".

"I still think our salvation lies in operating rooms. Incisions over the forehead, incisions in the heart. Removing those propensities for evil and destruction. Do you see what I mean?"

"Homo faber, the black light will say, now you are *sapiens*!"

"How can you be so sure about so much you cannot see?"

"*Bleed, Bleed, poor country.*
Great tyranny, lay thou thy basis sure,
For goodness dares not check thee."

"Is what him going on with now?"

"Stuck in his brain since him drop out of school: Shakespeare, like food particle in his teeth."

"Don't bother continue. It don't have no rhyme."

"Militarism in my blood? That's as ridiculous as, say, spiritualism in your blood."

"Had an uncle who fought to save Great Britain, and to preserve his love for Beethoven. I could see him now, squinting down the barrel of a rifle aimed at your uncle's helmeted head."

"I can't tell you 'cause I don't know what my uncle was thinking in 1934."

"*Bleed, poor island...*"

"Islands are bastard children squirming under the belt of their godfathers. Those angry gods! Those rum-gut fathers."

"Island-nations! Mainland-nations! Crude traps for the spirit, make I tell you."

"Ever hear how them tout this island to tourists: white sand, blue sky, hot-blooded black rhythms!"

"Then one day that hot blood gush and scald a tourist in the marketplace. Next thing you hear – a crime unprecedented in the island's history!"

"A rime unpresidented, his story on I land."

"Let the power fall on I."

"Embracing the black man, accepting his mind and body – the first act of love, the final revolution!"

"But I & I like how you express yourself: *Mine is the crisis of abundance.* Yes, truly. Too much, too little, same crisis!"

"It's just that I can't follow your vision all the way, your faith in redemption for us all. I fear, I honestly fear, that one way or another we'll all pass away and be forgotten. There will be always this horrible decaying present, not some divine presence, among us."

"Sin-ical, Rasta, sin-ical!"

"Don't make it sound like a betrayal."

"Bete royale, bete royale!"

"Cock/tale shaker! Why must you break up and mystify everything before we comprehend it?"

"Community? You and I talking, one and one – that is community! Hardest thing to build these days. Not enough silence, like mortar, to build with."

...and so flowed the rivers' discourse under bridges built by the Healing of the Nations. Then we all said, *Likkle more* or Goodnight.

It is possible to imagine conversations like this in any city, where there's a self-absorbed bourgeoisie, a student's union or a Parisian sidewalk cafe; and waiters who serve coffee and cognac, while an artist with a neatly clipped goatee removes the cellophane from a cigarette pack. What's different on this planet, in this crow's nest perch of a hill, is precisely that gift for prophecy (bolstered by the irrefutable evidence of chapter and verse), that tumorous certainty embedded in the Ras about Man's place in the universe.

...matters, as ponderous as whale blubber on the mind, which makes you long sometimes for the banality of *what terrible weather we're having* and *I have a dentist's appointment*.

A manic wish for relief nudged me coquettishly, you could say, towards Ikael.

He seemed the only one not shouldering some weighty cross of an obligation to decipher the universe, though there was nothing ephemeral about the smell of turpentine, the care he lavished on his brushes, his uncapped tubes tortured for every last drop of colour.

He had his own little shed adjoining the house, roofed with palm branches; I would wander over there to exchange a smile, share a *spliff*, study his landscapes and seascapes; trying not to appear too idle or intrusive, like a tourist peering over his shoulders, which always made him irritable.

I was curious about the painting he was working on, the new direction.

On the left of the canvas a space ship, its nose buried in the earth, fiery flame still burning at its upended base, and hundreds of arrows stuck in its frame like porcupine needles; in the centre the bredren sitting in a circle, naked, smoking the herb; on the right of the canvas a forest, another circle of men, the space crew, naked, smoking the herb; and two more naked men, Rasta & crew captain, standing close, staring up at a planet in the sky that could be Earth or the Moon.

Poor Ikael! Hauled away to the island prison when barely a youth for a crime he would never dream of committing; thrown into a cell like lamb's meat to starved carnivores; released later but not before he'd been pounced on by two inmates and buggered.

One morning, when grey clouds threatened to shut out the light for most of the day, I found him sprawled in his easy chair, an old car seat, looking uninspired or deflated; like someone to whom you might say in a marital living room, *You look as if you could use a drink*. I had nothing to offer except a *spliff*, and a sigh that was not yet a sign of boredom.

I felt a kitten's affection for him; I had come to admire his choice of solitude. Catching him like this, at loose ends, his obsessed-artist guard down, I felt an impulse to peek, to push open that door that was often firmly shut; get an eyeful of his privacies, items of obsession left lying around when his room didn't anticipate visitors.

I stepped inside. The room was much too dark.

"Want an orange?" he asked, out of the darkness.

"Thank you," I said.

We'd grown so comforted by a disdainful self-sufficiency, eating when we felt like it, saving our innermost feelings for those orgies of the spirit after sunset, we'd almost lost an predilection for commonplace courtesy, viewing such habits as perhaps dispiriting: clichés or banalities that ran like sewers through the marketplace: tools of deception and venality.

But here in a lapse of his painter's intensity was Ikael, a parachutist from *spliff*-puffed clouds, preparing to share an or-

ange with me, even as insects dived and flitted around us like
paper planes, and lizards chased each other in the undergrowth, and those forest birds kept up a street fair's din in the
trees, so much like the concourse of city traffic you try to sub-
sume under the tinkle of your spoon stirring sugar in a coffee
cup.

"There is something I've always wanted to ask you," I said.

"Ask I?" He could barely conceal his astonished delight.

"About your paintings," I continued recklessly.

I was watching with interest the movement of his hands as
he peeled the orange; the curious way the knife slid easily
through the skin, round and round – or was it the knife held
firmly in one hand while the other, the left hand, revolved the
orange? – so that you had the illusion of the skin paring away
at exactly the same point of contact between revolving orange
and firmly held knife.

Exactly the way someone should handle this spinning globe,
paring away all accretions harmful to the human spirit; scraping off with some cleansing knife all the dross and gloss –
though who would be the trusted surgeon?

"What about I paintings?" Ikael asked.

He was about to slice the orange in two cleanly balanced
halves. I stopped him. I took the orange and pulled it apart in
two rough sections, juice squirting in my eyes, and I offered
him the larger piece.

"Have you ever thought of holding an exhibition?" I asked.
"I mean, selecting the best canvasses and holding a show somewhere. In the marketplace, for instance."

He didn't answer me rightaway. He bit into the orange, spitting the seeds back into the soil. Then he said:

"Is a gift I man use. Discovered in a most humiliating way
while I & I was in gaol." He looked up, as if to make sure I'd

taken his meaning. "Some use drum and words; others wood or plastic. I man deal with the colours of the universe."

"It's just that, I was thinking..."

"You think too much... What you want to know is why I man make paintings nobody will ever see?"

"Are there places you can go to show your work? Art galleries?" I asked.

He laughed. "Is what you see around you in abundance, our natural wealth, colours, free from that imprisoning grey of winter. You see, the 'scapes hold the key to man's consciousness. The 'scapes could clear up all those paradoxes of being. I man paint toward that, same way you grope forward, like a baby on all fours, with innocent-fool questions."

Those last words stung me like the unexpected whip of a scorpion's tail; he hadn't meant to, but his words unlike his colours had a way of sometimes spinning out of control.

He looked at me, his face pleading for instant comprehension, his weary eyes filled to the brim with seascapes and landscapes. Then he shivered, as from a draft, a chill of caution in the air.

I drew near him; I put my arms around his shoulders; I felt his body shudder, as if discarding some skin of folly and regret.

Gently, firmly – a little embarrassed too – he shook my hands off and returned to those ample folds he had always known: distant rippling hills, the corrugated ocean surface, the chastening sun.

"Tell you a little something," he said. "You ever hear 'bout Neil Armstrong?"

"Who?"

"First man to walk on the moon. I man write to him – don't laugh – ask him to take a little vacation on this here island. Would meet him at the airport same way we meet you."

"I've heard of him. Why would you want him here?"

He was leaning forward, speaking not loudly, in a hoarse desperate tone, as if now that the cork had popped out of the bottle there was no holding back his next disclosure.

"Watch here, now! Neil Armstrong hold vital clues to man's place on this here planet. *Him was out there!* Through the window of his space capsule him one behold what I man struggle to perceive through I work: something him could never fully explain to scientists or newspapers or to his wife: something that invade his total being: a new sense of human proportion, a feeling for humankind that envelope him the moment him step out and behold: the Earth, that soap bubble, spinning outside his body. *See it?* Centuries of fighting and dying and procreating leading up: to that single step: that view, empowering and humbling: seeing ourselves from outside our selves: an event unparalleled since the Resurrection."

It was an effort of articulation he was perhaps uncomfortable with, preferring instead aphorisms, jokes, the strokings of his brush. I felt pinched with guilt. I had led him on, had drawn him into conversation, into blathering revelations that made him sound foolish in our eyes. He seemed to slump in his makeshift chair, from chagrin or a sense of futility or waste.

"Did you ever try using that theme in a painting? I mean, Man out there, the astronaut's personal vision..."

But it was useless pushing this conversation beyond the limits set by our clumsy foreplay, my hacking away at our frozen hungers, our sea-bed yearnings. Ikael was spent.

The spirit fuel of that moment had sent our bulkhead of unsureness to higher heights. There was now only a vibration trailing in the air, that billowing cloud at the base of the human spirit soaring as far up as it dare, before it fell back: a rhythm as timeless as sunrise and sunset; a vibration exploited in endless repetitions by our bodies in darkened rooms, ignoring cries of mercy from our souls.

"But when will we go down to the marketplace?"

It was dark outside; grasshoppers kept up a ragged chorus of lament or jubilation. We had settled in for the night, reclining in moods as personal as pyjamas; we smoked *the Healing of the Nations* and chased after great notions, as elusive as butterflies, with long stretches of silence during which Selassie, swinging gently in the hammock, seemed faraway, self-absorbed.

My question was meant for his ears. I'd posed it in a nonchalant throwaway manner, not wishing to hint again at that traveller's itchiness to do something: snap photographs or visit a local ruin: impulses that might unwittingly suggest I'd grown tired of his company.

"You and this marketplace!" Selassie muttered. "Babylon's sirens calling, making you long for certain dead habits, certain distractions." He was packing his chalice with herb.

"I would like to *see* it," I said.

"I man reveal to you the iniquity therein."

"I know. I understand. But all I have is *your* word. Some people like to swim a separate route to the same oceanic truth. It's the only real freedom left these days."

"Cho, rest yourself."

Sensing some contest of wills, Kilmanjaro put his hands behind his head like some eagle-eyed referee watching out for low blows or unfair tactics. Ikael wasn't likely to come to my support despite the encouraging smile he aimed at me.

"Sometimes," I pushed on, gamely, "I mistrust this view from the hill."

"What better place, what greater vantage point: a tiny island, a dot on the world map, a pimple on the flattened rump of this planet: what better spot – after the cotton wool swab and the needle check – to inject your meanings or sedatives."

"But what do we *do*?" I asked.

Selassie sat up as if the question had been followed by a stinging blow to his ears. To mask his irritation he glanced up at a portrait of His Imperial Majesty, Haile Selassie I which hung on a wall.

There were several portraits of H.I.M., along with carvings and the paintings by Ikael, which gave to the house the ambience of a miniature castle; the carvings and paintings like so much ancestral paraphernalia in a royal household. And where else on this planet could one find such courtly discourse and silence; where else but among these bearded aristocrats – though they would be the first to reject that claim, having gone to great lengths to cultivate an ordinariness of being.

"Is what we *not doing*," Selassie continued, his voice rising in operatic passion, "*not* peering enviously at our neighbours from the bunker of the skull; *not* mobilising the masses to march for freedom and hungrier days; *not* rubbing our palms and marvelling at landing crafts on the beaches, unloading cannibals, anthropologists, Eldorado-hunters – tourists of one description or another."

Suddenly he stiffened as if a voice that could have originated from the framed portrait of His Imperial Majesty had whispered a salutary note of restraint. He struck a match, lit up the chalice, and where once his head sat on the throne of his shoulders delivering sermons, there were exhalations of smoke, a swirling mist, through which his voice made one final pronouncement:

"Crack wide open the atom, but let the Healing of the Nations enter therein. *Selah*."

Then he walked out of the room.

And that was that; my proposal entertained and rejected; my audience with Selassie over.

In the silence, in the churned wake left by those propeller blades, I sensed the others awaiting my next move, perhaps anticipating a wheel-wrenching swerve: packing my bag in a huff and a puff, determined to prove I could survive outside all this, didn't need their patronage or escort, after all... and in any case...

"You looking thin these days," Kilmanjaro said, getting up to disperse any residue of illwill that hung in the air. The smile on his face was playful; it nudged me away from doubt and half-decision.

"Tell I man, how you see that bredren," Ikael said. He was referring to Selassie who might have been standing just outside the door contemplating distant stars.

In the mood I was in, the challenge and the chance to redress an imbalance proved irresistible.

"I'll tell you how I see him," I said, raising my voice, taking aim at the doorway. "I see him as some sort of Christ figure, nailed to his cross, only he seems cheerful about his fate since on either side of him, nailed up the same way, are his companions in spirit – Karl Marx and Haile Selassie."

"*Irie!*" Their laughter was like cheers of admiration for a view well framed.

"He is indifferent to the cheering crowds, the soldiers playing dice at his feet. He's above all that, in his separate world, chatting away merrily with these two, only they're dead or dying from overexposure, and sometimes I think he's not fully aware of that."

It was unheard of, this retort, this exposure; for the first time, it seemed, someone had held a mirror up to his imperial majesty – for I meant no personal insult to Selassie – that stripped him of ceremonial uniform and feathered helmet, that cut him down to some measurable mortal size.

This time the laughter and slow handclapping came from the door as Selassie, smiling like a chastened school boy, gave a mock salute, and said, all right, we would go down to the market place whenever it suited my pleasure; and no one felt happier than I at that delicate moment for an equilibrium of spirit had been restored.

The night before our journey to the marketplace I was unable to sleep; I lay as tense as a child buoyed by promises and picnic expectations; wondering what the market place looked like, how we'd get there.

This venture out also marked the resumption of that journey I'd started so many days or weeks before; I was faced therefore with the option of taking everything with me, of leaving the mansion on the hill... and then an airline office, return reservations and other obligations I didn't wish to face, not just yet, if at all; for I'd begun to dread this: the fall through the trapdoor, back into familiar places and habits, boredom and sadness, the rest of the (other) world sealed off except for a news flash on the transistor, things you read about in the newspapers, statistics of natural disaster, carnage, unimaginable agonies.

Just before daylight this thought occurred to me: if you chose to reject everything, what are you left with? If you simply gave it up, left it all back there waiting for you; staying here instead – or at least extending my stay on this (other) side of the planet – what then?

Nothing. To reconnect you. What then?

For the circumstances that housed my life here were extraordinary, beyond measure and dream: doing or not-doing (which was the same); manoeuvring through the world without the rudder of credit cards, ideological correctness, a lover's need; and, right at that moment, waiting for the morning light to crack like a starter's pistol, sending me off on an excursion into the forbidden and doomed side of the planet: the town centre of the North Coast.

It took us awhile to get moving. Judging from the early morning sun the day promised to be uninterruptedly clear; I was eager to start, fearing some bizarre shift in the mood of the heavens, a vengeful downpour, an abrupt cancellation of our plan, keeping us indoors.

Everyone was taking his time: scrubbing his teeth with sagebush, selecting the right pair of boots, the right tam, the right belt, searching for a walking stick; green, black, gold and red colour strips ornamenting everything; dark glasses, that touch of vanity or insulation; a hint of sulking reluctance from Selassie; a feeling of foreboding, as if this trip was something ill-advised, but a pledge had been made and, *hold on one second, forget to feed the goats them*; and *all right, time to make a move before we get arrested...*

Exhilarating, at first, to be walking along that road; the different shades of green on trees and vegetation, the rippling hills seen from different angles, the grass tickling your ankles.

We were compelled to walk in single file, Kilmanjaro striding in front, the rest of us following like a procession of pilgrims, wary of vehicles racing up behind us, though I was the only one to step aside, fearing I'd be sideswiped by drivers who always passed us at breakneck dust-swirling speed.

Soon I was looking over my shoulders, falling behind a little, running to catch up with the last man, Ikael. Now and then Selassie glanced back, catching my eye, seeming to laugh at the way I straggled.

Sky not quite so blue, clouds a little flaccid, but still a beautiful day in open country; cattle grazing in someone's fenced off property; a glimpse of tiny dwellings way back from the road.

I felt the dampness on my perspiring back; when next I caught up with Ikael, I asked him if it was at all possible to stop somewhere and rest; it would depend, he said, on the two indefatigable striders out front for whom this was no idle jaunt with time set aside to spread a table cloth on the grass and chew a sandwich.

My mood soured a little to one of irritation. Why did we have to do things the difficult way, the more punishing way: walking these interminable miles to the market place, when surely it was possible to flag down a bus or a taxi, or thumb a ride? And what would happen if my feet refused to take another step?

Always the road surface, ragged, crumbling at the edges. Occasionally a sight to behold: children fetching pails on their heads, turning around to stare after us; a man astride a donkey, his legs hanging down like unfair weights, the beast uncomplaining; then sudden bright showers of rain, for despite the presence of the sun we were drenched at intervals, the rain pelting down out of a clear sky as if summoned by the prayers of some parched region of earth, so that my clothes would be soaked one instant, dry the next.

Then I lost them. They'd disappeared around a bend, and it was easy to assume they had simply pulled ahead, leaving me to pick my way forward as best I could since this was all my idea, my obsession, and I would catch up if I wanted to, or fall to the ground from fatigue...

I saw the ocean. There was a path from the road through scrub and dry branches. I stumbled out onto the white sand and there they were, in various postures of meditation, long-haired sea lions at ease on the beach, drawing on the herb.

I fell on my knees wearily, and tried to dissolve my useless anger in the hiss of foamy waves collapsing in the sand.

Watching the curving coastline, the ocean swells racing up the beach was soothing for awhile, until Selassie, unable to resist an impulse to leave droppings of profundity right there on the sand declared:

"I man feel I know this place. Once in time long gone, I man was here. Exact same place and circumstance."

No one said anything. He turned to looked at me. He was quite serious. He started to repeat his observation but I cut him short.

"It's a feeling of *deja vue*," I said. "A mental phenomenon. The mind plays tricks like that."

"No trick, this. I man *know* this place; been here before."

"You must have been dreaming," I suggested coldly. "What else did you see? Yourself in white robes? Waiting for ships to take you across the ocean? To Ethiopia? The ocean plays tricks too."

He was leaning on his elbow, looking at me, puzzled no doubt by my petulant tone. Then he laughed, his teeth sparkling in the sun. He dived into his shoulder bag, came up with brown paper and started rolling a *spliff*.

I placed the knapsack under my head, drew up my knees and closed my eyes; I was trying to wish away all the tiredness in my bones; the suspicion, too, that I was in the grip of some island fever, for suddenly my body was on fire, and the wind coming off the ocean waves gave me shivers of trepidation.

Selassie was humming, which was his way of sharpening blades for some new dialectical thrust.

"*And when he had opened the third seal, I heard the third beast say, come and see. And I beheld, and lo a black horse; and he that sat on him had a pair of balances in his hand.*"

He put a flame to the *spliff* and was sucking it quickly to life.

"From the Book of Revelations," he said. "Truly, that was I man vision. Four in Issemble, on these white sands, preparing to mount black horses, to ride across the ocean, a pair of scales in I & I hands."

"Horsemen of the Apocalypse!" I said. "Was I one of them?"

"Cynical, incurably cynical! Dreaming is a vessel that ship man backward and forward through time. *You* can't see that, cause you fear the darkness of reckoning in 1945 – the bone-littered sea-bed, the grinning sharks waiting for you to capsize with your burden of guilt."

Which was unfair, a low blow, but right at that moment I was in no condition to consider even a modest protest.

"Here," he said, in an abrupt shift of mood, passing me the spliff. "Draw away and rest. We soon enter the marketplace."

With his fingers he tried to remove beads of fire from my brow. I opened my eyes and smiled my gratitude. There were strands of grey in his thick black beard; his face was soft and gentle, as if freed from all subversive desire; a face overripe with self-importance, too, a consequence of that sentinel's lonely perch on any rampart or hill.

Sleep was all I craved now, respite and a chance to sweat away the fever creeping over me.

I wanted to stay right there on the beach until the turning tide's crabbed fingers tickled my feet, advising me to stir. Nothing to worry about. I had the feeling that, come what may, I would never be deserted by the Ras, never be abandoned to the vagaries of tide or wind; this I imagined was as close as you could come in any paradise of the poor to a feeling of being valued and loved...

By the time we got to the market place my eyes were rivers of burning fever. I was drifting along strange backwaters where images of the Ras were like lilies on the surface: images of evenings outside our house under the tree, the sun imploding in silent miracles of colour, when it seemed we were waiting for the world to speak, to unclothe its secrets.

Now Selassie was saying, "Stay close. Don't get separated."

A pedestrian flung curses at an impatient motorist; neon made zigzag flashes in a shopping plaza; car horns blasted like Roman trumpets; young men in dark glasses, talking fast, flashing gold-ringed fingers, offered to guide anyone to places of illicit pleasure. We were a tight group of pilgrims shuffling along a street jammed with hucksters and hustlers (and the prettiest harlots) shoppers and strollers, planeloads of sun-eaters.

The market place! This was what I wanted so much to see, only now my watery eyes could make little solid sense of anything. The fever kept pouring that river through; my body shuddered, as if an ice cold hand had touched my spine in pity. At times I felt distinctly fish-eyed. My eyelids were heavy and they hurt whenever I opened and closed them.

Like a protective blanket the bredren drew close, sheltering me as we walked. Once we were violently jostled. I heard someone apologise in high falsetto. Ikael was saying something that came to me in fragments:

"This place peopled with possibilities... of being and having... servant could be master, master could be servant... natives mimic tourists... open-ended... Roman holiday ...the market supplies any flavour of human vice, pleasure or sacrifice... at the snap of your finger ...any service, once you have gold to trade..."

Rock guitars whining through a transistor going by; long hair, tinted glasses, odour of cannabis; half naked buttered bodies toasting on that hot white grille, the beach; sunshine-eaters who, in cities of glass and cancer, might have been ice cream vendors, aircraft mechanics, Chiefs of Staff, monks, marines and Maoists, nurses, secretaries, housewives...

"Couldn't we stop awhile?" I pleaded.

Ikael gripped my arm and helped me over to a table outside a sidewalk bar. Again, he said:

"Sometimes, weary of capital expansion, burdened by deposits of days and nights like carbon on the soul, there is a longing for a place to shed that waste, a primal place, in the remote backyards of cold cities. People throw themselves away; they suffer any humiliation, just to be here, just to be renewed, made light and whole again."

"Since when you full of words," Selassie said, getting up, touching himself as if his hip pocket had just been picked of black pearls.

Then he said to me in a conspiratorial whisper: "Don't be taken in by what you see and hear around you. Three-card man can spin words and images as magically as any shaman."

"So where you going?" Ikael asked.

"You don't see her condition? We have to find a way to restore her original state. Soon come."

Then he stalked off, followed by Kilmanjaro.

What was my condition? All of a sudden I wanted to see myself in a mirror (there was none at that palace of interiors, the house we occupied on the hill). I wanted to see my face one last time before it curled into cinders and was blown away, consumed by this raging fever.

What happened at this point I've had to reconstruct with a little help from Ikael; he was my saviour and witness; he reeled me in like a flounder from the turbulence of certain death; for I was sinking fast under the leaden certainty that I had been stricken by some obscure infection.

I remember dragging myself to my feet, trying to stand, knocking over a few chairs, lurching forward and wandering away through the crowds; though to hear Ikael tell it, I had apparently started off in pursuit of a face in the crowd I thought I'd recognised.

He was astonished; he tried to restrain me. I flailed my arms, shouting deliriously about pursuing the face or image in the crowd.

We began to attract attention. We became a sideshow of local madness, with people stopping to stare, or stepping out of my raving path; and Ikael trying not to appear as my tormentor in dread locks, pleading with me:

"Hold down! What you chasing you'll never catch. It will always elude you. I man know what you dealing with. Thousands take off from this island, possessed the same way: say them tracking and them tracking: far up into the cold North: chasing the ass-end of some missile: a scent to illusion. Just rest yourself here, the bredren soon come."

The end came when we stumbled upon a group of women singing; through my water-filled eyes I could see only their broad hips and bare feet; I could hear cowbells and drums and a moaning refrain from their lips; they swayed in a kind of half-moon motion; they clapped their hands.

I remember those jewels of brilliant light, their eyes reaching out of black faces, like stars of compassion you might perceive in a universe of weariness and pain.

They helped me to a table. I was babbling an old woman's God-fearing prayers, a young girl's man-loving screams, other hysterias. I raised my head and tried to grasp those points of light, to hold back those fast fading stars, before I passed away.

As for death, what happened, I used to imagine, was this: a gradual diminishing of the light, of all sound, as of a howling locomotive vanishing to a point of stillness and silence on the tracks; then suddenly a soft lovely darkness wherein one rested an indeterminate length of time. A waiting room.

I awoke one night to discover that the room was same one I had lived in on the hill, with the hammock, and the voices of the Ras in bible-based conversation. The difference was the water which filled the room right up to the ceiling.

I thought at first we had metamorphosed into subterranean creatures, albeit with human faces; that this was our transitional state while we awaited God's judgement. The water seemed very much our new element; it flowed through our eyes, our noses; it felt cold as it commingled with fluids in our bodies.

The bredren were in spirited conversation, their words emerging like so many tiny bubbles which burst to release their meaning.

I tried to move my body. Apart from my gross fish-eye, what must have been the rest of me felt solid, heavy; an encasement that had to be lifted before my soul could be free, for the bredren were speaking as if they were the only ones alive.

Once Selassie turned his head and looked in my direction. He seemed lost in thought. I could swear he looked right through me as if there was nothing there.

All I had the strength for was to lift those eyelids, feel them heave open like a steel trapdoor, then crash down when I couldn't hold them up longer.

Selassie was saying, his words coming to my ears in a ferocious stream of anger:

"Was the easiest task in the world since Christ fed fish to the thousands. Just walk away. Leave her to the mercy of the tourist board..."

"No, Rasta, couldn't do that," Ikael murmured.

"What you think she come here for? To lose herself!"

"Then, why you never ask her to leave from the beginning? Why bring her all this way, only to abandon her? Is something in yourself you fear, make you always want to ditch and run. Is a flight from your own humanity."

"Hear him, now," Selassie sniggered. "Self-taught artist turn amateur philosopher!"

He looked at Kilmanjaro who had his arms folded, his head lowered, half-listening to all this:

"Ever since him was a boy," Selassie continued, "you ask him to lose a stray puppy, just take him 'way and lose him; you want to see that puppy follow him back home. Is like him have some scent for souls vagrant and unsheltered."

"Vagrant like you, Rasta."

They fell silent. It didn't take long to realise they were talking about me, about something that should have happened or did happen.

"So what, then? Might as well hear the whole story," Selassie said.

"Well, she start walking away, like some memory in the wind calling to her. Walking away, and rambling in her mother tongue..."

"And you, following her, like some detective of the spirit... *Cho!*"

At this stage, no longer sure whether I was phantom or living flesh, hearing enough to persuade me that something irreversible had happened, I made a desperate attempt to get up, bent on intervening, on making my presence here known.

There was a burning sensation on my chest as I tried to move; the water made warps before my eyes; the bredren, still speaking, diminished or expanded into grotesque watery shapes.

I was sitting up. The next struggle was to stand and walk or wade toward the table. That proved too much for my leaden limbs. I fainted and fell back.

Ikael was leaning over me, pressing a damp rag on my forehead. My eyes were still ablaze with fever but I could make out lines of anxiety on his face.

"Is all right," he was saying, "just rest yourself. Fever hold you all the while but it look like it leaving now."

I don't think he heard me asking: *where am I, what happened, why were you talking about me as if I were dead?*

He slipped away, then returned with a cup of steaming liquid. "Herb tea. Drink. Will help drive away the fire." He held my shoulders until I'd drunk it all.

I tried once again to sit up. The last thing I sensed before falling once more into sleep was the aroma of *The Healing of the Nations*. Somewhere outside my vision, I knew, Selassie was drawing on the chalice and observing the curious drama of Ikael at my bedside, administering to my distress.

I don't know how long I lay there. Hours that might have slipped into days that might have melted into weeks. It could all have happened the same day and night. In brief moments of consciousness the tableau never changed: Ikael leaning over me, pouring liquid through my lips; light reflected on the bare ceiling; my limbs feeling as if they'd been fractured then simply glued back.

When it was over, when the fever and discomfort had vanished, when I was able to rise again from that watery grave, I expected everyone to hail my recovery, to greet me with smiles relief and delight. I came face to face with the most baffling indifference.

Ikael was absorbed in a new painting; he gave me the barest acknowledgement, a wave of the brush, and pointed me to the door, where perhaps a delegation with bouquets and embraces was waiting.

It had rained the night before. When I stepped outside I was held in thrall by the spray of morning light as from some golden shower head in the sky, the mist that hung over the valley, the glistening wetness of leaves, the damp soil which must have soaked up every inch of rainfall, like some parched throat near the driest death; and the grey, barely shimmering surface of the sea.

Once before I had knocked on the door of that waiting room, it didn't open, then out of nowhere men in white coats, with masks over their noses, dragged me away, pushed me back through a tunnel, into another room, where I lay for a while under a white sheet, with life-support systems, until another door opened, and more faces hovered over my life, familiar and strange faces, offering more support, and it was too much, too suffocating, all the tubes and emotion and support, turning me away to vague thoughts of other ways to shed old lives, irreversible ways to enter new kingdoms... as a nomad on a camel might ponder which way, in a city of skyscrapers and traffic lights, to turn ...which is confessing that as I walked step after step on that bare damp earth, through that freshly rinsed morning, I knew I had found it, that place in the universe that offered breath of vision, volts of new life; the "visitor from foreign" was now native to the Planet of Ras, the Planet of Ras was native to her quivering wet being... so that the bredren didn't have to welcome me back like an old friend and explorer; they had passed before through those rooms, tunnels, doors; they had discovered how ephemeral it is, this febrile home, this body, with its birthmarks and birthrights, its self-deluding orifices; they had pulled ahead; and as always, I lagged behind, still dragging fierce attachments, false premises, old expectations like a tattered blanket full of brilliant holes.

So this is where we are.

Something else needs to be removed, a sliver from a reddened heel, an explanation for those exasperated shoe salesmen, magistrates, caffeined intellectuals who insist.

A day in a department store when, still a child, I chose to disappear, to hide from my mother who was paying for a summer dress, while my father waited outside in the car; an impulse to play a game, there among the racks of summer dresses, so that one moment

    she was here, standing close to her mother's hem,

               and

the next I was nowhere to be found, despite the cries of my mother who must have thought I'd been abducted, for how else could she explain,   *as if she'd vanished into thin air*, she said to my father afterwards   absorbing to hear them searching everywhere, calling my name, while all I could see were the shoes of people walking by, pausing at the racks, of course I had to   *promise never to do that again, do you hear*? But only long after I'd discovered a world of shoes and ankles, stepping and crunching, that circled my singing heart without intruding, and I wished it could be like that forever, a lone, untroubled heart in a world of ankles and shoes, for sometimes people   parents, politicians, police act as if they owned the store, they panic and throw you in cells or wards once they realise they can't sell you, wear you like a shoe, dispose of you as they wish   so this is where I am, on the Planet of Ras; it could be anywhere once you've learned to shed that skin called nation-home, feel no longer compelled to take out of that trunk, for a good laugh or a cry, old costumes, jackets, skull caps, helmets, berets; frayed habits too tight for your expanding waist; century old resentments; pledged allegiance to flags; old loves.

    For where else can one locate an island of authentic feeling, if one resists that draft, refuses to join that march from Day 1 to 365 (bed to job, hand to mouth, bullet to chamber) dragging chains of hurts, regrets, unfinished vendettas?

    So much depends on catching up, closing that distance between myself and the Ras; our speaking with one heart though our cadence and syntax may vary, despite that impulse, during

consuming streaks of silence, to measure or name the counter-
points in our sound.

III

At my suggestion we secured a round table for our after sunset conversations. It prompted a few snide remarks about my
need for structure, a hint at colonial invaders who (anyone here
with memories of whiplash from the plantations would tell you)
brought with them an obsession with tea, verandas and cricket
pitches.

I intended, of course, to place among us a symbol of one-
ness, to encourage a pooling of our separate silences; to make
easier, too, the passing of that soup bowl from which we helped
ourselves, each according to his spiritual need, or in which we
placed some emotional tithe, the fruit of our daily labour. Despite more grumbling, that this might be the start of some imported distraction – a game of cards or seances – it worked.

"What lies on the South Coast?" I asked one evening, toss-
ing that question on the table like a rare coin, since conceiv-
ably there had to be some redeeming beauty or truth to balance the abhorrence of the marketplace.

"Take her there! Show her," Ikael, said laughing. "Her mind
wouldn't rest 'til the equation is complete."

"No more journeys out for I," Kilmanjaro chimed in.

Selassie sensing a trap snorted at the idea, giving me time
to find my own answers to conundrums, since any thought of
showing me around smacked of a relapse into role-playing.

"What's so problematic about showing me the South Coast?"
I asked. "And in any case we've played games before. Remember the night I arrived? When I saved you all from a terrible
bludgeoning by the local Gestapo. The authority of *the white
knight*, remember?

"*Irie*! Time to even up the score, Rasta," Ikael said.

Selassie was not amused. "Sound to me like the flip side of foolish dead ritual. This here life too important for playing games," he said.

"And you *saved us all!*" he continued, after a pause. "Sound to me like you forget conveniently a most recent rescue at sea, when someone's frail vessel went under, in raging flames, torpedoed by someone's blind desire."

"*Irie!*" Ikael said, winking at me, which was his signal to disengage, let the duellist swish at the air with his sword if he must, and leave the rest to silence, the play of humour, like a cat's paw, on the mind.

Selassie was away for most of the next day.

It was a warm dry day. I spoke to Kilmanjaro about the possibility of raising hens. We could do many things with eggs apart from eating them. He eyed me suspiciously, not sure what I meant, though he said he'd love the sound of cockcrows waking him in the morning.

Selassie returned just before sunset pushing a motorcycle. I saw him when he was half way up the hill. At first I could not believe my eyes; he had paused for a moment to mop his brow, measuring how much further he had to go. I ran down the hill thinking perhaps I could help. He waved me away and pushed the motorcycle all the way up.

"Where did you get this?" I asked.

"From the war museum," he said, irritably.

It did look like a relic from World War II, all handlebars and spokes and sturdy steel frame.

Selassie sat down, exhausted, as though he had pushed it all the way from memories of a battlefield in France or in 1945; he was in no mood for jest or idle questions.

Then Ikael wandered outside, saw this contraption, came closer, walked around it, studied it, touched the handlebars.

"All it need now is the sidecar," he declared, smiling at me.

Only then did it occur to me – the South Coast! We would after all be travelling to the South Coast, Selassie and I, on this motorcycle!

I struggled to compose myself, to project an image of restraint and nonchalance, not raising hopes or running up flags of high expectation.

Of course, it had to be worked on. I stayed out of the way as Selassie, putting aside the Bible, unearthing from somewhere a bag of tools, began tinkering with it.

One afternoon I ventured an aimless remark about auto mechanic skills I never knew he had – a road not taken? an old wound covered up? an ambition deferred? This set him ruminating, even as he seemed to work with deep concentration, on his high school days, and evil teachers who had steered him away from scholarly heights, pointing him instead to institutions where he could acquire useful vocational skills.

All of which I barely listened to since it was more intriguing to watch him as he tried to kick-start the machine, rising off the saddle, pushing down the starter, his ital body more used to the curve of the hammock; and the motorcycle making that wheezing asthmatic sound as of a life expiring, its body refusing service no matter how hard he kicked it.

But the day came when with a roar that belonged to technology a decade back the motorbike announced it would after all oblige; it would take us wherever we wanted to go.

A dusting of the seat, the foot rest extended, and we were off, sputtering and bouncing down the hill.

"So which way? What's the movement?" Selassie asked over his shoulder, when we came to the road.

"The South, my captain," I said.

"I could show you places of interest: shopping plazas, cinemas, suburbs, the university, a red light section. We are mimics in miniature: how you say, a *microcosm* of those cities of cold commerce; on the scruffy, half-finished side, but still..."

"I didn't come here to tour the island," I said, sensing this was some kind of test, a probing for residual motives.

"I don't know what you expect to find."

"Why not start, why not move in a generally south direction?" I said. "Let that movement take care of what we see".

He laughed and said, "Spoken like a true bredren who knows there is nothing left for man to discover. All is vanity and illusion: left-rightism, rich-poorism, top-bottomism: choose your side and weapons of destruction..."

It looked for a moment as if we'd never get moving, that Selassie had secured the motorbike, had reprised its serviceable life for the single purpose of demonstrating, as we sat in throbbing readiness, the futility of human progress, human curiosity.

"Do you think it will rain?" I asked, glancing up at the sky.

He followed my glance; he looked at me, as if he'd been tricked; he straightened his shoulders, revved the motorbike; and so began our plunge toward the South.

No sooner had we got underway – our stiff bodies leaning forward, our wind-sluiced faces wary of speed and bends and accidents – than it became apparent that the motorcycle had its own anxieties: how many miles was it expected to deliver in its reconditioned state to rider and pillion-mate? It served us early notice that, given the uneven roadway, and despite Selassie's coaxing hand on the throttle, there were limits to its extended life.

Dazzlingly blue sky: dry hillsides: dilapidated village shops; people in drab clothes staring after us; the navels of swollen bellies; dust and swaying overcrowded buses; perilous overtaking: with the passing of every mile stone it became clear we would not make it to the South coast; that as a compromise the South would have to meet us halfway on the road.

When eventually the motorcycle faltered signalling it had had enough, Selassie refused at first to believe it had given up the ghost.

We were coasting down a hilly road, grateful for any wind assistance when the motorcycle gave its last gasp, leaving us enough momentum to turn off the road and into an open field.

We got off. Selassie stood pondering his next move (he had left his tool kit behind). I looked around wondering vaguely where we were.

A group of boys, raggedy children, with dry hair and bony limbs were scuffling around a football, kicking up clouds of dust. It looked wide enough to be a playing field. At the other end, I saw hovering birds, a mountain of refuse, paper and litter bowled around by the wind. A field of refuse and waste.

And, as if to confirm my suspicion, a refuse disposal truck swung onto the field, scattering the ball players who then chased after the dust in its wake. The truck made a reckless U turn, stopped, backed up its rear end, released its load, then came charging back, bouncing and banging, at the ballplayers, scattering them again in a swirl of dust.

A field of destitution. Half naked boys (and now shapeless women) scratching and scavenging amidst great mounds of waste. Like pigs amidst great mounds of waste.

I stared with my astonished eye; it needed no explanation; the wind blew scraps of paper around our feet; the dust and the smell from the truck struck us like a wave. Selassie made a decorous cough, and with a despairing wave of his hand he started walking away. This was to be the final resting place of the motorcycle, he'd decided; a place it could rust away quietly (assuming the ball players didn't strip it for disposable parts first).

"Welcome to the South," he said, starting back up the road.

Running after him, glancing back until the field of refuse and its human scavengers had disappeared from view, I sensed a sullen anger in his stride, in his body pitched in forward motion like an out of luck hunter calling it a day, heading back to camp.

"Reduced to pigs, those people! What do they hope to find in all that refuse?" I said to him, trying to match his stride.

"Bottles of expensive cologne," he shouted back. "An economist's memo to the Prime Minister. The bald head of a CIA agent. Anything used, useless and useful again."

The journey back to the hill was exhausting, the sun unforgiving; often I fell behind; at several points on the road I stopped to rest my aching feet. Never once (though I was tempted to) did I raise my voice imploring him to wait for me. I knew what he was thinking: *I hope you're satisfied, catch up when you can.*

As we came up the hill – Kilmanjaro was chasing after a stray goat in the underbrush; the sun was slipping away surreptitiously – I felt he was perhaps more disturbed by this outing than his silence showed.

I was scraping sand and dirt from the soles of my sandals, and washing the dust from between my toes, when it occurred to me that perhaps something (residue from our contact with that other humanity – discarded, refused?) had somehow sneaked under our skin, under our neat metaphysical framings; like dust in our eyes it made for a troubling, grainy vision at least for awhile.

This was something we could explore as we rubbed our eyes – this profound discomfort we now felt, however well camouflaged.

Someone had thoughtfully prepared a pot of steaming soup, filled with vegetables; it was restorative as a hot tub. We ate in brooding silence, relieved that no one was in a mood to ask, *So how was the journey South?*

Later, after some desultory talk – Kilmanjaro's strange excitement over a new popular singer from the city whose records spoke of hardship among "the downpressed", whose name, he was convinced, would one day streak like a blazing comet across the firmament – after a sharing of *The Healing of the Nations*, then a decision by the others to turn in for the night, Selassie and I were left alone at the table.

At first, eschewing any roundtable discussing, he moved away to the hammock, where he busied himself packing herb. Struggling with my own uneasiness I stepped outside, and took calming gulps of night air.

A full moon was out in the sky. I couldn't help thinking how indifferently the light must fall upon cities with powerful street lights; upon mountains of the refused everywhere in the world: the human scavengers who dance or pray or smoke chillum pipes of old fictions under its transforming glow.

A gentle sea breeze had come ashore; the anonymous din of grasshoppers was suddenly a clear intrusive refrain.

I turned back inside; I could resolve nothing standing at the door, arms folded over my stomach, my back to the sullen vision-maker who at that moment was probably letting the tension out of his spiritual sack with deep inhalations.

He was sitting at the table; the Bible was open in front of him; he was twirling strands of his beard and turning pages with the nonchalance of a university professor, the Book requiring some kind of fresh intellectual engagement even though its contents had been poured over so many times like a manual for repairs to the spirit.

Still disgruntled, I couldn't resist a parting cheap shot, as I prepared to glide past him.

"Ah, *the tool kit*. Got some tinkering to do before you turn in?" He didn't look up. His fingers kept playing with his beard, ignoring or pretending to ignore my remark. "I know what King James says – *The meek shall inherit the earth*, but that does nothing for the wind pains cutting up their stomachs. I mean, how could we *not-concern* ourselves with them?"

We had crossed this field of human dilemma on many a night, our words like torchlights in that dark; and although the hot soup had spread its reassuring warmth inside our bodies, something else, gonads of raw anxiety inside our stomachs, now fought for some of the same soupy reassurance. It was doubtful, too, whether more and deeper inhalations of *The Healing of the Nations* could restore a sense of order to the turmoil inside our heads, the maelstrom inside our hearts.

Selassie sighed and looked up with the eyes of a befuddled man.

I was about to smile, a victor's cheap smile, when his hands turned the pages of the Bible to reveal – lying pressed like a dried flower – a clipping of yellowed newsprint. I was arrested. Like a too curious bystander I drew closer to the table, my face a flickering candle.

He was a man disoriented, and at that moment guilty of grave concealment. For what after all was a clipping of dead news doing amidst those eternal pages? And what – I found my heartbeat racing with excitement – did the clipping have to say to any Selassie of midnight certainties?

He gave a deep sigh and turned the Bible around so that the pages – somewhere in the Book of Revelation – and the clipping now faced me.

"A riddle as profound as those twin births from the same egg: Brandenburg Bach and the Belsen bakers," he said, leaning back, nudging me to go ahead, read:

His Imperial Majesty, Haile Selassie I, Emperor of Ethiopia,
King of Kings, Conquering Lion of Judah, arrived... yesterday
afternoon to a welcome of superlatives. And he wept. He cried
as he stood on the steps of an aircraft of Ethiopian Airlines...
and surveyed the vast and uncontrollable crowd which had
gathered. The tears welled up in his eyes and down his face.
And they brought with them thousands of colourful Ethiopian
flags and bunting, palm leaves, firecrackers, thunder bolts,
drums and the abeng... The cries were everywhere. The day has
come. God is with us. Let we touch the hem of his garment.

A momentous event, reported, it seemed, with a newspaper-
man's penchant for high drama and excitement. Yet underneath
it all, a powerful riddle, if one were to believe Selassie's head-
scratching babble.

I read the article again, focusing on the words he'd under-
lined, the phrases he drew my attention to; which hinted that
somehow the event, a ghostly yellowed thing of the past, had
taken root inside him, had spread thick vines on his stomach's
soft walls; and was at moments like this – what moment like
this? – a floating shard in the eye of his memory.

"An *attraction* at once physical and spiritual, repeated
through the centuries: the shaman and the tribe," he said. "Yet
when His Imperial Majesty step forward here, *tears roll down*
from his eyes. For whom did he cry?"

"Were you there? Did you see him" I asked.

"The crowd surged forward as he stepped out of that cabin
in the sky. I man feel that surge like some huge ocean swell
uplifting I vessel, sweeping I forward. I never tell this to a soul
but when I sight him there, I man was shaking like a leaf, weep-
ing like a child."

"It must have been a very moving occasion."

"Cho, stop mouthing words like some bored dinner guest!"

he snapped. "Next you'll be talking 'bout confession being good
for the soul!"

"I beg your pardon," I snapped back. "I'm not sure I understand ... calling this a riddle, when it looks more like a
straight case of private trauma, which I might not be righteously
qualified to diagnose. So go ahead, heal thyself, physician."

We fell silent. Like arms weary of broadswords our voices
were lowered for a while. I sensed Selassie retreating from his
own imperial instincts to a point where he was in all seriousness, as never before, asking me to help; to provide perhaps a
reading of the event from outside its time and place, since waiting for it to write its meanings inside him had evidently not
worked.

"What do you think he saw as he stepped off the plane?" I
asked tentatively.

He was thoughtful for awhile. Then he murmured, "Flags,
palm leaves, drums...."

"No beyond that. What did he see before him? A new con-
stituency? A state of grace? The gyrations of ruined souls?"

His fingers idly scuffed the surface of table; his face was
almost solemn under the cowl of his locks. He scratched himself and said, trying to sound relaxed:

"I man never really look at it that way... I begin to consider
how him *feel*, you know, maybe a shudder of recognition... as if
the weight of his imperial majesty – all the medals, the titles,
the impeccably tailored uniform – come like a vagrant's coat,
too heavy on his shoulders... So while them singing praises,
him *feel*... right there... like a tired old man, frail and tired... as
if all him really want now was solitude, not waving crowds; a
chair, a flower garden, evening newspapers, not a kingdom."

"But in *their* eyes, H.I.M. had arrived."

He lifted the *spliff* to his lips again, like a condemned man
asking for time.

This entire day of circumstance had taken its toll on him. Since the others, Ikael and Kilmanjaro, had retired, he could not resort to his usual evasive tricks: jokes that swept all ambivalences away, digressive puns, copulating rhymes. He looked all of a sudden like a sad grounded bird, its wings clipped; flights into zones of metaphysics were now out of the question; he would have to see this through, or shut the Bible and admit that this faded clipping was no more significant than a crossword puzzle.

"And why didn't Hirohito not once cry?" he declared.

"Hero- who?"

"That other Emperor, who gave to his adoring throngs the password – *Banzai!* – to eternal life."

"Seaweed caught in the propellers," I muttered.

"What is that?"

"I was thinking: you're like a man in a boat stalled in the middle of the ocean, and there's all this seaweed entangled in the propeller blades, and you keep diving, coming up for air, then diving to clear it away."

"You know," he said, a little testily, looking at me with herb-shot, distant eyes, "I don't think you understand how one man, one grizzled old pirate of a man – a man who like to lie in bed in his shorts scratching himself – him one could plunge a nation of millions into decades of suffering and grief. No, you can't deal with that considering the world out there to which you claim to be reconciled. Not to mention your running amnesia about events in 1934..."

"1934... amnesia...? I wasn't there, I told you. There is nothing for me to block out. Nothing."

"Convenient," he said, sitting back on his spine, and stretching his legs. "Just tear out the pages from 1934 on down; that way you don't feel responsible for anything before the day you were conceived. *Convenient*."

"Listen! We've ploughed and seeded this ground before. I told you I'd become reconciled to those pages, to that stain in our history. I'm not going to wear them like a hairshirt of guilt for the rest of my life."

He made a hissing sound through his teeth. In the state he was in he couldn't recognise his own inconsistencies if they shook bare buttocks in his face.

"Then, tell I man 'bout your Emperor, him with the pounding fist and the missing testicle. Can you see him crying?"

"Pity was not one of his strong points," I said. "There was nothing behind those eyes. Though, come to think of it, he may have had other things in common with the Emperor."

"What you mean?"

"Men of obsession. Solitary men, driven by some internal code or deprivation, some imagined slight or bruise... a cruel father."

"*Cho*, I bet him never smoke herb."

"No, that was beyond the bunker of his imagination."

"'Cause, from him smoke the herb, him would have had no use for all them rallies and torchlight parades, and fooling himself with *final solutions*."

Something else was happening beneath this heated reasoning, beneath the sparring of our emotions, the ebb and flow of anger, in a sense as absurd as when two people – Cain & Abel, Adam & Eve – find themselves arguing dangerously over nothing. I had never before felt so profoundly engaged with someone, as if the fish hook of his need had snagged me in the white underbelly, a need deeper than anything I had felt for and felt in any man. What remained now was the taut line, the undersea wriggle, the silver flash of the catch flapping in the net.

"My uncle," I said, calmly, deliberately, testing the line, "that helmeted target of your uncle's rifle, he said that in 1934, amidst the banners and flapping flags and the strutting symmetric formations, there were deep hungers, deep anguish, a desperate longing for a way out... *which is probably what those people were looking for in that field of waste...* but in any case, our peaked cap Emperor-King, if he ever once felt the need to cry, learnt instead to fill his eyes with visions of new nationhood. He simply took your breath away with that vision, my uncle said."

"Then, where was your uncle?"

"In the same position as you. Among the people lining the streets, his face in the crowd, his eyes in the fishbowl of his head."

Silence, again, for as long as it took the soldiers, crisp and polished, to strut past the gallery where His Imperial Majesty, tired but unrelentingly royal, was taking the salute.

"Want some more soup?" he asked.

"Thank you, I've had enough," I said.

On an impulse I got up and walked outside. It was perhaps a rude thing to do, but feelings like warning bells under my skin had imploded all over me. Not the heady feelings you associate with heady conversation. Something close to a powerful anxiety: fear mixed with quivering expectation: an anxiety about our tangled lives.

I heard him singing inside, fragments of a song, and then a meditative pause, as if it really didn't matter what I thought or felt; or maybe he had dipped his spoon into the steaming bowl of soup; all of which mattered to me at that moment (the fishhook still in my underbelly) even as I stretched myself on the ground and stared up at the heavens.

I was asking myself questions I'd cracked mirrors with before: *Who am I? Why do I keep throwing myself away? Why don't I feel as if I belong somewhere?* Except that, back then, they were razor blades aiming at my wrist, or capsules of sweet release sliding down my throat; now they were stones I'd picked up from the earth and was hurling at the smooth surface of the universe; now I thought I felt ripples on my heart.

Somehow I understood what was happening, like alterations in your heartpace you can't ignore, only I was afraid of making the old mistake: a banal gesture, those overused words of dissembling, the purge of a good night's sleep.

I felt his presence even before he stooped beside me and offered me the *spliff*, his fingers pinching the folded paper, his wrist gentle, firm; he was humming the song now as if respectful of my solitude, and following my gaze deep into the blue-black night.

"The serene sky, the outpouring of light every morning, each day's passover into night," I said, a little nervously, skipping on words as on stones in unsure water. "...the wind gambolling up from the sea... the aroma of limes, herb, ital-cooking... a Mecca for spirit-weary pilgrims; no, a place where my firmly planted heart can grasp anew its roots, the living truth of myself... in stones, wood, trees, birds, wind, ocean..."

"To say nothing 'bout the company you now keep."

"That, too!" I said, laughing, loving this new bare jocularity of speech.

"But it's really this place!" I said.

"Praise Jah!" he said.

"No, I'd rather praise you."

"No praises for I. You see't here, my life – simple, shorn of illusions, ambition's rash, the itching fingers of commerce..."

"Though you must admit, a lot depends on your *not-moving*, not crossing certain boundaries. You're a stationary man, Rasta!" I said.

My mood was playful; my spirit was testing new wings.

"Stationary, I? You mean, man have technology, so man must travel. Tools forging paths to new kinds of ignorance and colonization: profit lust, marriage bust: the planting of flags

rather than *The Healing of the Nations*: a feeling of being useful and used: cannon fodder or chemical waste for diminutive
emperors everywhere."

He stopped, overcome by a fit of coughing, his forehead crinkled. It was as if in that outburst of phlegm he'd been pulled
up short by a crushing blow on the shell of his chest, like a
signal or a warning from inside its walls about the impulse to
rhetorical overexertion.

I slapped his back and offered to get him a glass of water.
He shook his finger at me, forbidding so banal a gesture. I
would have none of it this time. I held the cup to his lips and
urged him to drink, open wide that crack of self-sufficiency.

Afterwards I sat closer to him. He picked up a stick and in
an idle obsessed way he began digging furrows in the soil. He
was struggling, I knew, to recollect himself. When he spoke
again, his voice had lost some of its customary hectoring edge.

"Talk about not-crossing boundaries," he said, clearing his
throat, "hear I now: *You* coming *here* was the most important
journey I man ever made. Truly."

Bewildered, sensing we were about to tear away on some
freshly cut tract, I steeled myself and held on.

"Crossing that no-man's land whenever I sight I – that is
the real adventure: fraught with peril and possibility: the only
ground of community. Most people look away, or grab and bag
trophy for mantelpiece display, or drape themselves in ethnic
costume, or place a ring of ownership on the adoring other's
finger, or make stiff penetrations into the hole then jump ship...
and since you staring at I like I was some guru from Gurujati..."

"No, no!" I said, reaching out, touching his arm, "Sometimes I wish I could record what you say."

"*Cho*! Folly, that! Like leftovers from dinner conversation.
You must then clear away a load of words, which could turn
into a credo or a theory after you wash the dishes, then an evan-

gelical impulse come morning to do something for the be-
nighted masses."

"That's not what I mean. We could lose all the ground we've
seeded with questions today. By tomorrow, who knows, there
might be answers, frail buds."

"*Cho*, it will evaporate anyway, if you talking 'bout the warm
feeling in your stomach – nourished by the soup, which by the
way taste *irie* – or that *wish this night would never end*. which
every student intellectual is privileged to feel."

"Sin-ical, sinical," I said, wagging a finger. "When the winter frost stamps hard on the earth, the seeds of spring stir, get
ready for the coming thaw."

It was a throwaway remark, meant to cover a swelling confusion; my stomach was on fire; my head was lowered, staring
into a pool of silence. Suddenly I was aware of his gaze fixed
on me as if my face were melting before his eyes.

I looked up; he seemed a little self-conscious and unsure,
like someone in command who had finally doffed his hat and
was reviewing a march past of the world with a startlingly bare
rumpled head.

"The coming thaw..." he said; his fingers plucked a blade
of grass. "I man must deal still with that gordian knot inside,
that quest or question for I time, which the trembling fingers of
H.I.M. can't seem to loosen. A precondition for living. Or not-
living."

He had spoken with the gentlest concern and understanding
of what was churning inside him. All I could do just then was
smile and nod my head.

He stretched his arms and yawned, acknowledging fatigue
had caught up with him, with us; for it had been a long day
tunnelling into its labial night, and we were exhausted, after
pushing towards something still unformed, that would reveal
itself in its own time.

"Likkle more," he said.

"Yes, time for me to turn in too," I said.

"I & I can't promise, like a cap-'n-gowned professor, that *we'll continue this next time*. Besides right now..."

"Right now – sleep. You have an appointment in the morning!"

"*Cho*, you can stay right there," he said, with a wide boyish grin, "romancing the sea and the moon... and the centipedes."

"*Cho*," the sound bounced from my heart, though not in the way he usually said it, that Sisyphean carefree way of cold shouldering the blind stone of the world.

The following morning I awoke with the feeling that something was not quite right. The sun was pouring through every aperture and crack. I heard voices outside, unfamiliar sounds, feet crunching the leaves and grass. I got up and rushed to the door.

There were four men outside. When they saw me, their mouths fell open. Two of the men, clean-shaven official types, wore neat, tightfitting suits; one was a police officer with a red sash running down his serge trousers and a rifle held loosely at his side. The other man, red faced and rotund, was mopping his brow with a large white handkerchief and wiping the soles of his shoes in the grass.

Selassie appeared from around the side of the house. He carried a staff and might have been returning from an early morning stroll in the hills. The men turned and stared at him; they stared at me; they exchanged quizzical glances.

"Who are you? What are you doing here?" one of them said, stepping forward.

I rushed to join Selassie, standing by his side.

"Who are *you*? What are *you* doing here?" we shot back, speaking from one heart.

WHAT HAPPENING THERE, PRASH?

"Every morning when he got up Hat would sit on the ban-
nister of his back garden and shout across, *What happening
there, Bogart?*"

– V.S. Naipaul (*Miguel Street*)

"You don't start over things in life," he said wisely, "you
just have to go on from where you stop. Is not as if you born all
over again."

– Samuel Selvon (*A Brighter Sun*)

WHAT HAPPENING THERE, PRASH?

Prash was waiting for the end of his world. He was sitting in front of the television set in a half-furnished room in the Bronx N.Y.

The set was relaying horrible news of robbery, murder and bad weather but he wasn't really listening; it played at loud volume because he couldn't stand the silence dangling like a hangman's noose in his apartment. It was a late hour in the afternoon, though given the time of year – winter, the sky indifferent to the passage of the sun, the window blinds closed, the ceiling lights burning – it could have been day or night in his new world.

He was waiting for his wife to come home. There were a number of things he wanted to tell her.

At any moment there would be a knock on the door. It could the Police and the Super wanting to talk with him.

His eyes touched every object in the room: the three-piece living room set bought on layaway, a transistor radio, framed pictures of his wife's family. *Where do you go? Whom do you turn to when trouble, big trouble, hanging on to the balls of your life?*

He tried to relax. He pulled at his crotch and, like the starboy in a Western saloon, the big iron on his hip, waiting for Big Bad News to crash through the swing doors, he stretched out his legs in nonchalant readiness.

There would be a knock on the door. This is what he would do: he would get up, moving *cool* and slow, like Jack Palance in *Shane* getting off his horse to ladle water while he smiling at Alan Ladd; and he would open the door.

There might be two police officers with orange-coloured moustaches and cold blue eyes and loud American voices; and the skinny Super with a limp from Vietnam, who peppered his conversation with that sweet-sounding word *muddafukka*, who'd point a long finger and identify him; and maybe that wicked boy they called *Jaws* with silver braces in his teeth.

They would start asking him questions, lots of questions. He wasn't certain what he would say, how he would react. It could be the end of the world for him. But he could handle that.

I ready for them, all o' them, he shouted at the news reporter speaking to him from the television monitor. He wasn't sure he could deal with *this*:

1. Fits and Starts

One morning you wake up, fowl cocks crowing to the symphonic light of dawn, music from your neighbour's radio, somebody already up in the kitchen scratching their buttocks, breaking wind; and the country you live in has begun its first day as a Socialist Republic.

It made little difference to Prash what the city politicians were saying about the new man, the new society, the new time. People had to get to work. People needed taxis (the Government-owned bus system was as unreliable as the Government).

Prash was a taxi driver.

His wife stayed home to look after the house and their piece of land and the children.

Next morning you wake up, the fowl cocks still crowing, but

now chicken getting expensive, gasoline getting expensive; and spare parts for the taxi hard to obtain because – so the city politicians say – of *the serious foreign exchange situation*. But the people still had to get to work. The people needed taxis.

Prash was a mechanical wizard.

How he improvised to keep that taxi running would have astonished manufacturers from Detroit to Tokyo.

You wake up in the middle of the night, eyes wide, pain squeezing your chest like an accordion; these days your wife beginning to complain, you can't get back to sleep; this married life not working out; strange things happening everywhere; power cuts plunging the nation night after night into darkness and early pyjamas; and people grumbling and migrating because they have no power at all.

"Man, what we going do?" Sookmoon said in high-pitched distress. From the day they got married she called him *Man*. Prash took it as a measure of respect and devotion.

"You know, all I hearing from you these days is *nag, nag, nag*," Prash said.

"Man, neighbour say you can't get a job after you leave school unless you sign up for National Service. She say they does take advantage of Indians in the camps. Suppose something happen to these children. Suppose some black boy do something to Ameena."

"These children *not* going to no National Service. Moolchand not going! Ameena not going! They think coolie people stupid. Let them carry on with their foolishness."

Damn right! You are the man in the house. You can't let this place, you can't let any country, get you down. And country people not stupid!

"Listen, starting tomorrow we planting up the back yard. I buying a fork this weekend. We go grow tomato, lettuce, ochro, bora – everything we could plant. Moolchand must do some

weeding on weekends. And I getting a watering can for you.
What we don't eat, we go sell."

For a while the situation was under control. Sookmoon
watered the plants with devotion. Moolchand nearly chopped
off the toes on his left foot while weeding one weekend.
Whatever foolishness possessed the socialists in the city, they
were mistaken if they thought country people would lie down
and take it just like that!

Then Prash had another idea.

His taxi travelled the route from the ferry stelling to the city.
The Government-owned bus service had a bus schedule for the
same route. His new idea was to change his route: he would
run from the airport to the city.

His rumshop pardners, Whappee and Errol, couldn't figure
out this move. The purpose, he explained, was simple: *American dollars!*

"American dollars? But Prash, no American tourists coming here," Whappee said.

"And besides, nobody bringing in American money," Errol
said.

"And besides you going use up more gas going to the airport," Errol said.

Prash smiled and wagged his index finger: "You fellows
don't understand nothing. The Government say we have a serious foreign exchange situation. Is only one way for we people
to deal with that. We have to exchange we currency for foreign
dollars."

Sookmoon didn't like the new idea either.

"Man, we better off saving up we own money," she said. In
times of crisis, her response was usually to save up; things were
bound to get worse before they got better.

Prash told her, "Look, leave this situation to me. I know what
I doing."

And with that he stepped boldly into the black market.

He began working the airport route. He charged incoming visitors in U.S. dollars for the ride into the city; it always sounded like a bargain, and strangers knew little or nothing about the rate of exchange. He found that trading was heavy; there were buyers and sellers everywhere; at Christmas fellows walked the streets waving thick wads of currency like shak-shak.

The situation was under control.

You come home late one night, vexed to the world; the Government rig the elections again and people in the rumshop, people in the villages, people everywhere outside the city full of bitter disappointment and rage.

These days Sookmoon complaining more than ever; she saying how Moolchand not weeding the garden in the backyard: "He only complaining 'bout blisters on his hand from the cutlass, and how the sun too hot"; and Ameena staying out late at night with some young man.

Prash was the man in the house; he didn't have to put up with any slackness; he could take off his belt and lash their behinds. But all of a sudden, one evening, a strange silence and irritability came over him; he found himself brooding over his age (he had passed forty); and he felt a sharp need, like a pain in the behind, to be eased of all these problems, all these tiny manly responsibilities.

Hours before he had been stopped by a traffic cop. This happened on occasion; they pulled him over for speeding or overload. Sometimes he talked himself free; sometimes he passed a bribe. This time something happened that was like a donkey's kick to his soul.

The traffic cop took his time getting off the bike. He looked disgruntled and perspired behind fancy dark glasses. He was

wearing brand new serge fabric and black boots and he walked
in a manner that advertised his better-off status.

Black sonofabitch, Prash thought. He waited.

"What's happening there, comrade?" he said, trying to read
the officer's mood and intentions.

The officer mopped his face with a large white handkerchief;
he had a terrible razor rash under his chin; he walked around
the car, peered in; then he tapped his ballpoint on the sideview
mirror and declared, "All systems are go!"

He ignored Prash's protestations and wrote him a ticket for
carrying too many passengers and for reckless speeding.

For the first time in his life Prash felt broken, his manly
courage snapped like a twig, his taximan smarts unable to protect him. The world was suddenly a threatening place; it was
run by city people who wore smart uniforms made of newly
imported fabrics, who spoke in a strange code language (what
the hell did he mean by *All systems are go*?) For the first time
in his life his bones rattled with a countryman's fear.

That same evening Sookmoon stayed up waiting for him;
heated up the curry, set the table and waited for him. Prash
took the first mouthful. Then:

"Man, you hear what they doing now? They banning split
peas from the country. They know we can't make dhalpurri
without split peas and still they banning it!"

Sookmoon's shrill tone suggested a state of emergency. It
was a cry for help, for drastic action, for some display of shock
and indignation. To her dismay Prash just sat there unruffled,
chewing thoughtfully, as if the food in his mouth was at that
moment giving him cause for concern.

He had heard her, but shards of anxiety floating inside him
from the incident that morning still caused him worry and pain.
He said nothing. He was giving himself time to heal.

Usually Prash heard about crises and developments long before Sookmoon announced them. In his taxi every day he picked up people who slipped easily into a camaraderie of despair; he listened to heavy-hearted tales and frightening rumours; he heard the most amazing schemes for beating the food shortages. And he considered himself one of the few people who knew what was at the bottom of all this socialism.

In the rumshop on the main road he was the bearer of news from the city. Whappee and Errol, canefield workers, unfamiliar with the city, looked to him for predictions of what *them jackasses in the city* would do next to imperil their lives.

When he came home he pretended he was hearing everything Sookmoon said for the first time. It gave him the chance to think, to announce some new scheme in defence of his family. Besides, he sensed that Sookmoon took a strange pleasure in announcing the latest bad news.

For her part Sookmoon saw the Republic as a place in which they were victims of racial wickedness hatched in the city. When Prash gave orders, charting a new course of action, she was ready to play her part, making deep sacrifices to keep the family from sinking.

That night as he ate and drank, as he belched and called for another serving, as that meal seemed more like the last supper of its kind before the ban on split peas came into effect, Prash was silently admitting to himself that he had been sent reeling to the canvas.

He had given the Republic a good strong fight, using his wits to outsmart them; he had taken everything them bandits threw at him – devaluation, shortages, spare parts, power cuts, food lines. But this morning's occurrences, and then the news about the banning of split peas (a piece of information he was hearing for the first time) was like a kick in his groin, one hell of a blow!

Sookmoon waited and waited; she cleared away the dishes; she went inside the bedroom and waited some more; she asked Prash, "What wrong with you? How you so quiet?"

Prash climbed in beside her and gave a deep sigh; he stared up at the ceiling for a long time; then just as Sookmoon was drifting off to sleep, he announced, in barely a whisper, as if speaking to himself, "We have to get out of this country."

2. Finding A Way Out

It was probably the most anguished decision of his life. Once he had made it, or whispered it fearfully like a prayer, he wasn't sure what to do next, where to go. He told himself he needed time to conceive a plan of action. He watched events closely. He listened.

People were leaving the Republic every day. Somehow they got around the currency restrictions, the visa problem, the income tax office; somehow they boarded planes or boats and took off.

Prash drove many of them to the airport. Sometimes he was hired to transport whole families from the city. They sat squeezed up in the taxi, a sullen worried lot; they fussed about who going in this car, who going in the other car; the fortunate travellers received last minute instructions, and checked their travel folders over and over in case they'd left something behind.

Prash drove his taxi and smiled benevolently, minding his own business.

At the airport, watching scenes of desperation and quiet hope, he felt sorry for them – these city people, taking their chances in America, *voting with their feet*; they sounded brave and clever and full of wild hope. Secretly he considered them fools, pitiful fools; cutting loose, their canoes adrift now in the world, with no property, no stake in the country like the rice farmers, the *coolie people* they despised.

Now that he himself was thinking of leaving, his feelings toward them were more ambivalent.

In the rumshop he tried to steer the conversation towards migration.

Errol said, "You know Ramgolall? He end up in Trinidad. I hear he catching hell in that place."

Whappee said, "They does treat you like cowshit in them islands. From the moment you reach the airport, they threatening to run you out the place."

Errol wondered aloud if Prash was thinking of running.

"*Thinking of what*? And have people use me like horse manure? Lemme tell you something: I born here. Is here I go die."

And though he'd never given any thought to dying, he was suddenly disturbed at the thought of spending the rest of his entire life in the Republic.

So it was with a troubled mind that he announced one Sunday afternoon to his family, "We definitely leaving this country."

Moolchand and Ameena were excited; they waited to hear more.

Prash said, "We definitely leaving this cowshit country!"

Sookmoon heaved a deep worried sigh.

She had heard him that first night the notion was born. Tight-lipped, she swept the house, poking the broom into corners and under chairs, her head lowered in furious concentration. Then:

"Man, you crazy. We have no place to go. Besides, neighbour say they treating we people like criminals in the islands. At least here I have my piece of land and my pride. Allyou can go, I staying right here."

It was another blow to his soul, a second kick to his groin: to be reminded that the house, the piece of land, was the dowry from her family; to have no concrete plan to follow his decision. He felt soaked to the skin with shame.

For weeks after he was sullen and crotchety; often he came home drunk; Ameena and Moolchand stayed out of his way.

Sookmoon was patient; she tried to ignore his bad moods; she still watered the back garden; she felt a little guilty for not giving her husband support even if his ideas were crazy; she hoped his torment like a fever would eventually run its course.

Then something unexpected and fortuitous happened.

Cleaning out his taxi one Sunday he noticed something on the floor, two magazines rolled up and held by a rubber band, the pages evidently unread; probably left behind by one of his airport passengers: SEARS catalogue, GOOD HOUSEKEEPING. He called Ameena and gave them to her; she looked through them briefly, then gave them to Sookmoon; they disappeared and Prash thought nothing of it, until one afternoon he discovered them under his bed, the edges of the pages curled; he smiled; Sookmoon had begun to dream.

"Like you planning to buy new furniture for the house. Some things you get only in America," he teased. Sookmoon said nothing. "From now on I go ask the passengers if they bring any magazines."

Slowly the tide turned. As she leafed through the pages in her disgruntled way, Sookmoon's disinterest began to dissolve; she grumbled anew about the state of the country; she expressed dark fears of starvation and racial battles. She revealed that people in neighbouring villages were moving lock, stock and barrel to America; and Ameena was still threatened with the prospect of National Service.

"Neighbour say these days you must have a Party card if you want a good job."

One night, as Prash was getting ready to make love to her, she declared out of the blue, as if trying to disrobe herself of a troubling thought, "But, Man, if we leave this country, where we going stay?"

Prash hesitated for just one second, his desire suddenly stronger, sharper.

"Look, leave this situation to me. I go fix everything," he whispered in his most amorous voice. His fingers strayed up her thighs.

She slapped away his hands and crossed her legs. She couldn't understand how he could be thinking of *this* and at the same time wanting *that*.

"You have a sister in New York? Why you don't write she?" she asked him sharply.

"Why *you* don't write she?" Prash shot back.

Ameena wrote Prash's sister in New York; she expressed the family's interest in flying up – for a vacation, *not to stay*.

Two months passed with no reply.

Ameena wrote again explaining their need for an invitation or sponsorship. A letter eventually came from New York. The address sticker on the envelope had the name C.Gail Baker. It took them a while, before opening the letter, to figure out it was from Prash's sister, and that she had changed her name. In America she was no longer Champa Gilbacca.

The letter wasn't too welcoming in tone; it hinted at risks and serious penalties; it promised to do what it could, and it asked for more details.

Prash and Sookmoon now surprised each other with disclosures of their secret preparations.

Sookmoon had somehow secured all the paperwork the Embassy required; Prash revealed that he was saving American currency instead of selling it on the black market. Ameena and Moolchand were sworn to secrecy about their plans, though Moolchand was already wearing a sweatshirt with the BOSTON CELTICS logo.

More letters to New York. Trips to the Embassy in Prash's taxi (which didn't go unnoticed by the neighbours). Many months of uncertainty; deep distrust of employees at the Post Office; a brief loss of contact with New York; visits to various offices in the city. Another visit to the Embassy – the official was highly suspicious of Prash's intentions and wanted more statements from New York. Champa balked at having to reveal her financial status. More clouds of uncertainty. A perilous trip to the airline office with a paper bag of full of currency in rubber bands. Until the only problem left before their final departure, almost twelve months later, was what to do with the house and the taxi.

"We go leave it. We go lock up everything and leave it right here."

"Man, is what you saying? How long we going for?"

"We buying return tickets. We supposed to stay 21 days, but we could stay 21 weeks or 21 months. We could find work, make some Yankee dollars, come back here and we set up for life."

"But the children mightn't want to come back."

"Well, they could stay. Besides they getting old enough to start out on their own."

Sookmoon wasn't happy with this plan; it was asking her to give up property on solid ground for castles in the cold North American air; she pestered Prash with questions; she wanted more details.

"See what I mean?" Prash declared testily. "We ent even leave this country yet, and you start complaining! What you worried about? I tell you, wait till we get there first, things go work themselves out."

"Man, you crazy," Sookmoon said, giggling mischievously, a playful sound Prash hadn't heard in a long time, which he easily mistook for a surging new intimacy in their lives.

3. Time's Woof

When Prash thought of his sister in New York, which wasn't often, the word that brought a picture to mind was "disgrace". Other family members used other words – "wild", "pariah dog" – to conjure up more hate-filled images.

Champa herself, when pressed to explain the vagaries of her life, would flash the word "precocious"; she'd begin to describe her life growing up in her village; then she would declare with a theatrical wave of her hand, "Really, I was a precocious child." That statement was meant to cover up boring details, to explain away the many difficulties she later faced.

But what had she done to deserve her family's abiding wrath?

Upon leaving high school she had taken a job in the civil service (at that time the National Service idea had not yet been conceived). Word soon got back to the village that she had rented a house in the city and, to their great horror, was living alone; she encouraged no visitors, except a mysterious black man, high up in Government circles who, her family was convinced, was using her like a whore.

One Sunday afternoon the family (minus Prash) travelled to the city, hoping to persuade her to return to family and decency. They stood in her living room, relieved that the black man was not there; they pleaded and scolded; they wandered into the bedroom, pulled out handkerchiefs and dabbed their eyes. When she refused to be moved, they cursed her to a future of indescribable calamity, and told her that from that moment on she had no home.

Though summarily banished from their hearts, she was nevertheless not far from their minds. News about her kept filtering back to the village.

Ameena was the one who kept her household informed. She broke the news that Champa had left for New York; the black

man had been posted to the Embassy there and had recom-
mended Champa's secondment as a secretary. This news
caused some excitement, but deepened that image of her as a
"pariah dog".

The years went by. The last bit of news, before Ameena's
letters renewed contact, spoke of her taking college courses;
the black man had resigned his Embassy posting, and had left
his wife. Champa still worked with the Embassy; she lived
alone; she was still seeing him; amazingly she had avoided
pregnancy, which was the last breath of scandal everyone back
home waited for.

How did Prash feel as he waited for her in the airport lobby
(she was late; it was late September; they were shivering in
their new but inappropriate travel clothes)?

Right at that moment, he felt admiration for her courage,
her fearlessness; traits of character he imagined their people
needed back home to overthrow the Government, or at least to
escape its clutches.

Though he'd never given much thought to her life, falling in
line with the general disapproval of her behaviour, it now
seemed to him – as he rubbed his cold hands and wondered
where the hell she was – that Champa was also damn smart:
working her way into the Government, she had flown the coop;
she was free.

And as for all that talk about the black man using her, maybe
it was the other way around: maybe she was using him!

When Champa came through the sliding doors, he recognised her instantly despite all those years. He saw the little
sister he'd ignored, then envied after she'd won a scholarship
to a city high school; he saw the same skinny body, the flat
chest, the same blemished face which convinced him that, despite the rumours, no man, not even a black man could have

found her sexually attractive; he felt relief that she had shown up, that they would now get moving into the streets of America.

Champa heard someone call her name and she was startled; she turned to find her brother and his family waiting to embrace her. A grimace of unease darkened her face; they looked so pathetic, huddling and trembling, suitcases at their feet. Her brother's smile seemed foolishly earnest, his sky-blue suit badly tailored.

She wasn't sure what to say to them, but remembering she was now C.Gail Baker, she smiled awkwardly, and said:

"Oh, there you are. How is everybody? Did you have a nice trip?"

"We thought you wasn't coming," Prash said, reaching for the bags.

"I was caught in traffic, crawling for miles. Then when I got here I couldn't find anywhere to park near the entrance. The security people keep telling you to move on. Then this guy, he sounded Jamaican, said he'd let me park if I hurried in and got my party quickly, so come on, let's *get back to the car*."

That bright rush of words, the invitation to get back to the car, dispelled any awkwardness, and for the time being erased all old fears and suspicions. They hurried out of the lobby to the car.

Prash liked the way she seemed to take over their destiny, supervising every detail: where they sat, how to arrange the bags in the trunk; he liked the way she handled the Jamaican baggage man who grumbled about his tip; he admired her confidence at the wheel of this brand new expensive-looking machine.

Impressed by Champa's flow of words (embellished by her American accent) Prash couldn't resist pinching Sookmoon beside him in the back seat and nodding with pride at his sister.

For her part Sookmoon sat quietly, looking through the window, keeping her anxieties to herself. She was a little intimi-

dated by the tilt of Champa's head, the frizzy modern way she
wore her hair; she relaxed only when Champa, slipping into an
accent from back home, declared, "But allyou come up with
packed suitcases. Like allyou planning to stay for good." At
which point Sookmoon laughed nervously; she felt that Champa
wasn't so snobbish after all.

Champa's arrangements for their stay, though not elaborate,
had been thorough; she explained that with her college classes
and her job she had little time for leisure; they could use her
apartment for the duration of their stay; she had arranged to
stay with friends; she would drop by as often as time allowed.

She showed no interest in news or gossip about the family
nor the state of the country. The constant bright rush of words
hinted at the unremitting urgency of life in America.

That first night, as Moolchand and Ameena sat outside
watching late-night television, Prash and Sookmoon retired to
their bedroom.

"So how you like America?" Prash asked.

"It cold. We have to buy jackets and coats tomorrow."

"Well, a little *sweetness* now could warm you up nice," Prash
said, snuggling up to her bottom.

"Man, I tired. We been travelling since morning. Besides
this is Champa's bed"

"But we in America, now. This call for a little celebration."

"When we get our own bed we could celebrate."

And for the first time in a long while Prash turned away from
his wife, rebuffed and unsatiated. He got out of bed and ordered
Ameena and Moolchand to switch off the television. They gave
him looks of pure hatred. When he got back inside Sookmoon
was snoring.

His first night in America, and Prash lay wide awake, his
right hand consoling his crotch; bare hours in the city, and al-

ready he missed his taxi, his own bed, Mukerjee on the radio
foreday morning, Whappee and Errol, the rumshop on the main
road; all the village routines that once made him feel like a
swami in the tiny kingdom of his world.

4. Finding A Way To Stay

That first week in the city passed quickly and heavenly; they
ventured out in daily sorties through the streets, down into the
subway station, past the shelves of department stores. They
returned laden with shopping bags, startling the tenants of their
building as they crowded into the elevator.

They discovered the street bazaar of 14th Street and bought
themselves winter coats. Prash spent an hour in a makeshift
changing room trying on blue denims and boots, and popping
out every five minutes to ask Sookmoon, *How this look?*
Eventually losing patience she told him, "Man, just buy any
pants! I go take in the waist!" Ameena complained she was
tired of eating at McDonalds where she was sure everybody
was staring at them. They got lost in the subway and rode the
trains for hours before Prash found the courage to ask someone
for directions.

During the second week Prash came down with a cold and
stayed home. Despite warnings, Moolchand went out on his own
to the cinema. He returned after midnight, explaining he had
found an American friend who had taken him to 42nd Street.
Prash threatened to lock him out if he did it again. "You could
go sleep with your American friend."

Sookmoon found a shop that sold curry, not *Indi Madras*
curry from back home; curry in a green tin from India; they
had their first homecooked meal. She also discovered the *I Love
Lucy* show and planned the rest of her day around T.V. Guide
listings.

Champa showed up almost every day despite her busy schedule; she found the apartment, thanks to Sookmoon's vigilance, in not much disarray. She commented on the family purchases, offered advice on places to see, trains to take, bargains to pursue; then she grabbed her bag, some books, some clothing and disappeared.

One morning, in the middle of the *I Love Lucy* show (Ameena and Moolchand had gone out) Prash appeared in the living room, blowing his nose, a box of Kleenex tissue in his hand; he was naked from the waist down and displayed an enormous erection; in an unusually humble voice he asked Sookmoon to come inside. Sookmoon thought immediately of her Uncle Basdeo who lived in Canada. She sighed and went inside.

Afterwards she said to him, "Man, the money running out. What we going do?"

"Who say it running out?" Prash said, his old irritable self restored.

"We can't stay here forever. Champa acting nice, but soon she go want back her place."

"You hear she say anything? She complain to anybody?"

"Man, if we staying, we have to find a house. Besides Ameena talking 'bout going to school. These children have to finish their education."

"Look, leave everything to me. I go talk to Champa."

"You don't know this sister of yours. After all these years, you think she want family to burden her life now? Yesterday she was grumbling 'bout the electricity bill. I not waiting for anybody to kick me out their house."

Prash didn't answer. Sookmoon went back to the living room. The I Love Lucy show had ended. She put on her coat and without another word to Prash she left the apartment.

She returned late in the evening to find Prash still in pyjamas and in a state of frenzy.

"Where you been all day? You walk out the place, don't tell nobody where you going! No food in the house! You come back with your long empty hands. Not even Kentucky Fried Chicken! What the rass you think it is?"

Sookmoon calmly removed her coat. These outbursts of profanity, familiar and ignored back home, like the earlier display of naked lust, struck her as bad-mannered and out of order in a New York apartment.

"Just look at the mess you make with the peanut shell. On this *good good* carpet," she said.

"Wasn't for these peanuts I would be a skeleton by now."

"And hush your noise. Why you couldn't heat up some Campbell's soup. Besides, we have plenty apples."

"Campbell's watery soup...? Scrungy ice apples...? Look, find yourself in the kitchen and fix something fast."

Sookmoon dropped a card on the bed beside him and went into the kitchen.

Prash came storming out after her, waving the card:

"And what is this? Who is this *Pandit of Real Estate*?"

"He say he could find we a house. He say he could fix up everything: social security card, driver's licence, everything we need,if we staying here. But it going cost money."

"I ent spending a blind cent on some crook calling himself *Pandit of Real Estate*."

That night Prash was more belligerent; he sent Moolchand out to buy a six-pack of beer *at the corner shop*; he argued over keys, and people coming and going as they please; at one stage he slapped Ameena for answering back; his final show of authority was to declare, *No T.V. tonight for nobody*. He ordered everyone to bed.

Throughout all this Sookmoon was the essence of forbearance. Ever conscious of their presence in the apartment as guests, she was worried about keeping everything not theirs unbroken, intact, or as undisturbed as when they first arrived. She felt Prash needed to change his attitude; he was in America now; for some reason he had ceased to look ahead, to plan ahead; she had to talk to him.

She heard him outside singing Hindi songs from Indian movies; she heard him belch; she heard when he knocked a glass over and she worried lest he'd spilled beer on the couch. She was not afraid of him; just a little sad and embarrassed for his sake.

When he came inside the bedroom she pretended to be half-asleep, but she knew Prash was not finished.

He shut the door; he turned her over; he pulled and tore at her underwear; and like a wounded beast thrashing around in her undergrowth he expended the residue of that night's rage into her unprotesting body.

The following morning she left his breakfast covered in the oven; she shook his shoulder (he was hacking and coughing like a sick man confined to bed) and told him she was going out, taking Ameena and Moolchand with her.

They were gone for long hours.

They returned to a scene that paralysed them as they opened the door: Prash and Champa in what seemed a fierce inconsolable quarrel; Champa ostensibly arranging things in her apartment, and repeating, "Is time allyou move on."

Sookmoon was so upset she trembled and cried quietly; Prash looked dishevelled, unshaven and (judging from his slurring speech) drunk; she tried to determine what had caused this breakdown in relations.

Champa called Prash a bum; Prash called Champa a whore. Sookmoon cringed and pleaded with Prash to stop.

Her eye fell on a polished table where one of Prash's beer bottles had left a circular stain; she had warned Prash about using coasters; she now rebuked him loudly for his careless low-class ways.

Champa kept saying in aggrieved, angry tones, "I've been living without family all these years; nobody going to complicate my life now. *I don't need this shit!*"

When the shame and distress proved too much for her Sookmoon declared apologetically: "Is all right Champa. We moving out tomorrow. We find a place to stay."

This announcement brought shock and sobriety to Prash's face.

"Oh? *A place to stay?* Who say we staying anywhere? Lemme tell allyou something: I taking the next plane back home. Allyou could stay here if you want. Let the cold freeze off your backside! Let Immigration catch you and throw allyou backside in gaol!"

5. *In the Beginning*

Faced with seemingly intractable problems, Prash acted like a magician pulling scarves out of sleeves; he came up with ideas and schemes that caused his family and his friends to marvel at his smartness.

These ideas he picked up at the wheel of the taxi where passengers, responding to the unrelenting hardships in the Republic, vented their spleen at the Government and devised the most amazing schemes for survival.

Prash greeted and encouraged talk of these schemes with loud anarchic laughter, showing all his gold teeth; the passengers, feeling comforted and safe, came up with more inventive, even dangerous ideas.

In New York, with no taxi, faced with new dilemmas, Prash was more than a little lost for ideas. Nonetheless, he held fast to the belief that things would work themselves out, given time, and a little bit of luck. In fact, he'd always thought of America as a country where things were bound to get better, no matter how badly off you were when first you set foot on its streets.

Land of opportunity! You took your chances! When things got tough, you played it cool; you waited for the tide to turn.

When the family moved to the apartment in the Bronx, Prash felt, as he'd known all along, that the tide had turned.

If anyone was giving thought to the circumstances of the family, it was Sookmoon. Despite that image of the subdued and sacrificial wife (the result of premarital admonitions from her mother) she was always thinking of ways to make her family more secure.

Her high school education was followed aimlessly by courses in secretarial work; she was never bright and she couldn't see a future climbing limb by limb up the tree of some city profession. So when her mother announced she had found a husband for her – a man ten years older! – she was troubled at first, but she quickly resolved to do her best in that institution, the way she'd promised her mother to do her best at school exams.

She found a way to keep her mother-in-law at bay; she brought Ameena and Moolchand into the world; she managed to tame Prash's sexual urges which had threatened to keep her swollen and uncomfortable year after year. And though she complained often to Prash, it was meant as a gesture of deference to him as the man in the house; once she'd divined his true purpose, she got to work finding ways to support him. She liked doing things on the sly, and surprising him with the results.

Coming to America was in part inspired by her concern for Ameena, who was troublesome and headstrong as a child, bright in school, and different – she liked American Country and Western music, and had a pen pal in Ireland. For her Sookmoon felt there must be more than the socialist Republic could provide, with its national service and those predatory cadets. For Ameena, there had to be a whole new world.

She worried too that Ameena might one day abandon the family and run away, as Champa did, to the city. Once there, it took just one giant headstrong leap out of the Republic for her to be lost in the labyrinths of the world.

In the streets of New York, she'd begun to notice the way Ameena idled in front of store windows, or lagged behind as the family followed Prash's uncertain lead across busy intersections. Only days in the city, and already she felt Ameena slipping away.

The apartment in the Bronx was a stroke of good fortune, a lucky break; it would never have happened had she stayed in Champa's place, waiting patiently, allowing Prash time to chart their new course; it could only have happened by her stepping outside, seizing the moment, placing herself boldly and gamely in fortune's way.

6. Way to Go

"So tell me, where you get money to rent this place? To buy fridge and gas stove?"

"The stove and fridge come with the apartment. So they do it here," Sookmoon explained.

"And tell me, where we going sleep? On the bare floor?"

"We could buy three beds right now. They have a store round the corner, selling little fold-up beds, on *layaway*."

"On *what*?"

Sookmoon felt pleased with herself as she answered his questions; she spoke in a mildly respectful tone, soothing Prash's disgruntled manner; she hoped it would make him feel like the man still in charge.

She led the expedition to the store; she signed the receipts for the beds; Prash prowled the showroom sour-facedly examining and testing other items of furniture. He thought the store clerk, chewing gum and wearing a jacket and tie, looked like someone from the canefields of the Republic. He tried to flush him out by asking in a soft friendly tone, "How soon allyou go deliver the beds?" Not looking up, the man scribbled furiously on his receipt pad and said, his accent unshakeably American, "We could get these beds to you within 24 hours, sir!" Outside on the sidewalk Prash expressed loud misgivings about the quality of all the merchandise he had seen in the store.

When they returned home Sookmoon made another announcement. She had found a job.

"Is a long story," she said with a shy smile, turning away from their astonished faces.

Moolchand sucked his teeth, refusing to believe her. Only Ameena seemed delighted at the news.

She told Prash the story as they lay on their new bed (which sagged a little in the middle). He folded his arms and listened in grim silence. For the first time in his life he found himself receiving from his wife a lesson on how to survive.

Sookmoon had kept her ears and eyes open from the moment they'd boarded the plane; she had overheard Ameena talking to Champa; Moolchand had got some tips from his American friend on 42nd Street. Patching everything together, she had woven some sort of hasty quilt of tactics for making it in America.

She never fully explained how she'd found *The Pandit of Real Estate*; nor how she came upon the white lady in Manhattan who had hired her to look after her apartment.

"You mean, you going to work as *a maid*?" Prash asked, astonished, outraged, turning on his side to look at her.

Sensing anger and objection, she hastened to explain, with interspersed giggles, that she was *working*. Not as *a maid*. She was a household worker. The pay was good. And the lady had a little boy.

"She ask me if I had references. I tell her I come from Bhopal in India, and I had five children, all dead now. I been looking after them all my life until the accident kill them. They died crying for their mooma... She forget about the references."

Prash lay on his back staring at the ceiling. He couldn't believe what he was hearing; he didn't know how to respond to what he was hearing.

"She want things done a certain way, but she and me *clicking*. Everything working out fine."

Prash scratched his dry skin in an idle irritable way trying to absorb this new audacious side of Sookmoon, this dangerous bareface lying side of Sookmoon.

"You have to show teeth and lie," Sookmoon went on. "They like when you speak nice, and dress decent... I tell her I could cook Indian food real good. Right away she want to hire me..."

Prash felt his spirit run aground. He wanted to argue, but he was still looking forward to a night of *sweetness* in the new bed.

Her story finished, Sookmoon turned on her side – the warrior woman who had done a hard day's work finding a job and must now rest.

Prash was paralysed. He muttered aloud about no heat in the apartment, and somebody in the apartment above moving furniture around. Sookmoon didn't answer.

He sucked his teeth and told himself, "Is lucky she lucky". After all, he was the one who had brought them to America; and what she was now finding out – how to smile and lie – he had known about that long ago. In some ways when it came to survival, the car-cluttered streets of America were no different from the lily-choked canals of the Republic.

"You taking up too much of the blanket," he fretted, tugging fiercely at the covers.

"Is a *comforter*, not a blanket," Sookmoon said, gently, drowsily. "A *comforter*."

7. *Show Teeth and Lie*

The following morning, out of the corner of his eye, he saw Sookmoon getting dressed.

"Where you going?" he asked.

"I have to go to work," she replied.

"Already? You starting today?"

"Besides, Ameena and Moolchand have to get enrolled in a high school. School start at eight o'clock."

It was cold; he was under no obligation to get out of bed; he squirmed under the covers, sucking his teeth in disbelief and anger.

Sookmoon was simply responding to a need to nail down new routines and responsibilities as quickly as possible: the children in a school, Prash in a job, once he got off his behind and started looking; herself, armed with a subway map, setting off to work in Manhattan.

Prash slept until after midday.

He woke up, startled by the emptiness of the apartment, but he felt warm; he checked his watch and was surprised at how quickly time flew. He stared at the sleeves of the heater and wondered how the system worked throughout the building.

For an hour he stood at a window in his pyjamas observing the habits of a squirrel. He had never seen a squirrel before; he was fascinated by its bushy tail, the way it climbed walls and bare trees, so solitary and self-sufficient, impervious to the vagaries of the weather.

He wandered into the kitchen, scratching his belly.

When suddenly it felt as if someone had thrown a switch and turned off the heat in the building, he cursed loudly, looking up at the ceiling; then he crawled under the covers and went back to sleep.

The next morning, determined to be part of the bustle and preparation, he awoke early and was first in the bathroom; the others hammered on the door and told him to hurry up. Sookmoon asked him where he was going.

He said, "You think is you alone have business to take care of?"

Within a week Sookmoon had worked out her routines. She came home round about seven bursting with tales of another day in America. Ameena and Moolchand were enrolled in a High School. "They give Moolchand a test and they putting him in some Special Education program."

Moolchand was sulky and said very little when asked about the program. Ameena surprised everyone by revealing she'd found a part-time job as a cashier at a supermarket nearby; she went there after school, and brought home fliers with cut-out coupons for savings.

It was left now to Prash to find *something*, to pull his weight.

That morning he left the apartment; his intention was to check out the scene.

He was alarmed at the number of black people and Spanish-speaking people, evidently not working, aimlessly walking the streets; he put a little sway in his shoulders and tried to walk as if he was just passing through the neighbourhood. Still he felt uneasy; he felt surrounded by them.

Distances were greater and more exhausting than they seemed; people cursed at the slightest provocation; the graffiti on walls, the litter in the streets, broken glass on the sidewalk made him feel this was a neighbourhood as dangerous as the wild West.

All of which he reported to the family when they returned that night; the only reaction was from Sookmoon who asked casually, as she took off her coat, if he'd found a job.

"Wait, you think jobs does grow on trees?" he flared up in sulphurous anger.

His explorations continued for several days; each time he ventured two more blocks beyond the point he'd stopped the day before; always he returned home weary, watery-eyed and cold, with nothing to report.

Then one morning he discovered Jaggernathsingh.

He'd been walking past this solitary man, sitting on a bench, his face ashy and melancholy, a folded paper in his lap; one morning he thought he knew who the fellow was despite his hat, the scarf and the layers of winter clothes.

"Guess who I see today?" Prash announced that night, holding back his news, waiting for them to guess.

Nobody showed interest. "The man from the Rice Marketing Corporation... the embezzler... the man the Government looking for... say he going on long leave, then BAM he disappear with all the Corporation money... *Jaggernathsingh!*"

There was a long pause. Sookmoon asked, "What he doing in New York? I thought he was in Canada."

Disappointed with this response, Prash decided never to mention Jaggernathsingh's name again.

The next day he walked up to him, pointed his finger and said jokily, "I know you from somewhere." Jaggernathsingh gave him a suspicious stare, and then said, "What's happening, Comrade?" He looked jowly and overweight, with dark half-moons under his eyes.

They became fast friends. They met every day punctually at eleven o'clock; they talked; they watched the world go by like retired civil servants.

They talked about the alien new city and the sinking old Republic; Jaggernathsingh expressed bitterness at the socialists back home whose only interest – he repeated this, like the smutty last line of a calypso – was *in the broad asses of the people.*

Prash laughed; he pulled at his crotch and told Jaggernathsingh he hadn't laughed so good since he was in America.

They talked of power cuts and food prices, of dictators and democracy. Never once did the subject of the Rice Marketing Corporation or what they used to do back home come up.

This sharing of company, day after day, this respect for each man's secrets, each man's hidden purpose here in America was something new and comforting to Prash. He would have liked it to go on forever; but he had to return every night to Sookmoon, who now sighed often, and dropped remarks about rent and bills to pay.

When eventually he found his first job, the circumstances might have made for exciting retelling; he kept the story to himself.

He had waved across the street to Jaggernathsingh and was waiting for the lights to change when this taxi drove past, its doors splashed and dirty with dried slush; on its bumper, a telephone number, and the words, DRIVERS WANTED.

Prash dashed recklessly across the street and asked Jaggernathsingh for a ballpoint and notepaper. He found a public telephone booth, called the people; they gave him directions; and with little explanation, he bid a hasty farewell to Jaggernathsingh.

The Manager asked him few questions. Prash assured him he knew New York city like the back of his hand.

There was another man waiting to be interviewed, thin-faced and moustachioed, speaking in halting English; he told Prash he was from the Soviet Union. A smiling Prash, a man with a job, advised him, "Don't worry, Comrade. Just show teeth and lie."

That night when Sookmoon came home, carrying a large Woolworth shopping bag and heaving weary sighs, Prash said in a deliberately flat voice: "This America is a funny place.

Today I meet a man from Russia. He is a medical doctor. He can't find doctor work so now he driving taxi. Both of we starting out tomorrow. Funny place, this America."

Sookmoon's breathing and heartbeat must have stopped for two seconds. Then:

"Is time you stop calling people *Comrade*," she said, heading for the kitchen.

8. *The Man They Call Prash*

Once he'd started on the taxi job, Prash caught a glimpse of his future; it was as clear and simple as a rainbow; he would make big money quickly and, following his original tentative plan, go back home (with a barrel of spare parts) a self-sufficient man.

He and the Russian met the following morning and decided to share the same route, noncompetitively. Since their unfamiliar names made for difficult pronunciation, they decided to call each other, abbreviatedly, Pepski and Prash; they embraced over this decision like true comrades.

The Russian, who knew a little more about the Bronx, suggested they prowl or park near the exits of the subway station at 161st Street, where weary subway riders anxious to get home would be easy fares.

It would be a smart thing too, the Russian suggested, to follow the street over which the elevated subway tracks ran; wait until the passengers directed them to turn left or right. That way, guided by passenger directions, they could find their way around and back to the elevated tracks with little trouble.

There were other taxi-drivers at the 161st subway station: Africans, dark-skinned and amiable; Spanish-speaking drivers who were surly and resentful, and gestured in that menacing American way.

The first week went by smoothly, if not profitably; Prash had to make a few rapid adjustments: passengers had to be prodded for directions; they protested when he stopped along the route to pick up other people, preferring solitary rides to their destinations.

He discovered, too, that after mandatory deductions, he was left with very little take-home pay.

"In this country when you working for other people, is slave wage you getting," he grumbled to Sookmoon.

"*Eh-heh*," she said, not withholding or offering sympathy.

More problems arose when in an effort to increase his take-home pay, he ventured beyond boundaries of the familiar into the jungly derelict unknown.

He started picking up fares at random on his return to the subway stop; people asked sometimes to be taken to faraway strange areas; frequently he got lost; once he found himself quite suddenly merging onto, then rolling along, a three-lane highway that ran for miles into beautiful countryside. Trying to read the overhead green signs, he braked and slowed and panicked when tyres squealed behind him. He used up much gas money finding his way back to the subway.

"This place have plenty street signs, but the roads could run you straight to the North Pole," he said to Sookmoon.

"*Eh-heh*," she said, leaving subway and bus route maps conspicuously on the bed.

Then came the day of the dragon, that contest of courage and will which all newcomers to the city eventually face and must win before they move on.

He had stopped to pick up a chubby-faced young woman with a bawling child and a bulging plastic bag; she had trouble getting into the back seat; something snagged the bag; it ripped and its contents – the young woman's, the baby's clothing – threatened to spill everywhere.

"Something back here ripped my bag," the woman declared

even as she told him where to take her. "Fucking old rusty taxi... and I don't want no damn Spanish music on the radio... What you going to do about my bag?"

Prash was thrown into confusion; he kept looking back to catch a glimpse of the ripped bag; at the same time he was trying to read the street signs; he remembered what his Russian friend had told him about handling street emergencies: *Never admit it's your fault. Defend yourself with obscenities.* He was, however, overwhelmed by the woman's loud relentless fury. Then:

"Where the fuck you taking me? ...I told you *Undercliff Avenue*... Where the fuck you taking me?"

Panic rumbling in his bowels, he went through a red light. Braking, winding down his window, he called out to two men walking by, heads bowed into the cold wind:

"Hey, buddy, how you get to Undercliff Avenue from here?"

"What do I look like, some fucking information desk?" one man replied. They kept on walking.

"I'm getting out here," the young woman suddenly announced, fighting with the door handle. "You foreigners come to this country, take jobs away from people who born and grow here, and you don't know shit about this place... *not shit about this place*... And look what you done to my bag. I aint paying you shit..."

Feeling helpless, wanting at least to be paid for bringing her this far, knowing he must find his way back, and fed up with all the shit thrown unkindly at him, Prash let loose a short burst of his own: "You black muddahrass thiefing bitch!"

With that he drove angrily away.

The dragon was not yet finished with him.

Somewhere along a street of derelict buildings, he discovered the car was overheating; his idling speed was harsh. He stopped the car and opened the hood. Out of nowhere three fellows appeared, hands in pockets, their heads hooded. "How

you doing, my man, look like you got a little problem here."
They took turns peering at the engine.

Though they sounded friendly, they made Prash nervous.
"Is all right, I can fix it, no problem, no problem," he said
firmly, discouragingly.

The three men looked at him as if they'd done nothing and
didn't deserve his answering tone. Prash tried to smile. The
fellows turned and walked away.

Seconds later, his head still under the hood, he sensed
someone watching him; he glanced sideways, saw the blue side
of a police car; caught the unsmiling eyes of the two officers
watching him, paleface sheriffs of suspicion; in the pit of his
stomach fresh panic, fear of questions, fear of further investi-
gation, fear of discovery.

He shut down the hood; he waved to the officers. "It's okay,
boss! Everything under control!" He started the car and drove
away.

He returned the taxi quietly to the garage; he handed in his
receipts; he had lost more than just a day's pay; he had lost his
nerve, like a right arm, to the jaws of happenstance roaming
the streets. Not for him, not anymore, driving taxi in the city.

"If you working in this country, you have to look in too many
directions," he muttered to himself. The thought was like a
tourniquet to his fractured spirit.

He went home; he felt miserable; he longed for those hot
grungy days back in the Republic; he consoled himself by
putting away with workmanlike efficiency a six-pack of beer.
For a while, recalling his daredevil skills on the roads of the
Republic, he thought of going back to work the next day, taking the taxi out, showing drivers what a *coolie man* could do on
American highways.

That night he said nothing to Sookmoon; he lay staring up
at the ceiling. Once he shook her shoulder and complained

about her loud snoring. He felt cold and beaten; more than ever now, like a thirst for revenge, he wanted a job.

Not wishing to arouse suspicion, he left the house each day as if he was still at work. Walking the streets, his jobless condition now exposed to passing cars and trucks, to indifferent glances from people going about their business – all of this deepened his unhappiness.

A well-dressed couple smiled and offered him a religious tract. He read the caption – *Life in a Peaceful New World*.

"Why the hell you don't get a real job, eh?" he shouted at them. He put the tract away in his pocket, fearful of violating any littering law.

It dawned on him that other people were seeing him in different, less flattering ways. A lost soul. A scheming alien. A bum!

One day he found his way back to the company of Jaggernathsingh still sitting in his favourite spot, despite the deepening cold.

"How things, Comrade?" Prash hailed him, as if he'd just returned from a short vacation.

Jaggernathsingh smiled and said, "The man they call Prash!" He sounded like a loyal friend who had heard the news about Prash's recent exploits, and was proud and happy to share his leisure with so gallant a man.

9. You Get What You See

Prash was now not sure what to make of Jaggernathsingh. They met regularly round about midday at what Jaggernathsingh described as *my favourite first-class restaurant*; it offered Chinese and Spanish food and, working on his friendship with the manager, Jaggernathsingh was trying to introduce an Indian cuisine to the menu. He spoke of this idea to Prash one day as they waited to be served, lowering his voice to levels of controlled excitement.

Prash nodded, interrupting only to declare Jaggernathsingh a first-class genius; he chewed slowly, making a noticeable effort to listen; as they got ready to leave, he made a fuss about sharing the bill; invariably Jaggernathsingh stopped him with raised palm, told him it had been taken care of.

What was he to make of this man? Thief? Embezzler? National disgrace?

Prash was willing to forgive him his past if indeed he had stolen money from the Government. After all it was common knowledge that the Government, the city socialists, was stealing money from the people, off *the broad asses of the people.*

As they sat in the restaurant – both men evidently not working, yet eating very well – questions he wanted to ask came nervously to Prash's fingertips; he drummed on the table and scratched his arm; he decided to keep his questions to himself, not wishing to cause a tear in Jaggernathsingh's new image of leisure and largesse.

"You're one hell of a man," Prash declared, responding to another of Jaggernathsingh's ideas.

This one had to do with citizenship status for Indians who had fled the socialist regime. It seemed so simple. Russian Jews fleeing persecution in the Soviet Union, coming here, were no different from Indians fleeing the socialist regime back home.

"We have a case, man. A straight case of racial and communist oppression. Think about it," Jaggernathsingh said.

Prash belched, apologised and nodded. He told himself he would test the idea on Sookmoon.

Caught in a situation where he could not match Jaggernathsingh's generosity, he soon began to envy the man his neat attire, his privacy, his easy living. There were days when he stayed away, then returned, to determine whether his company was missed and valued.

He changed his image, giving up the blue denims and the cowboy boots, switching for a while to shoes and seamed trousers and an office man's sweater. It made him feel more like a man of substance as he walked the streets. Some people stepped out of his way.

"People does look at you like dog in this place," he heard himself saying one day.

Jaggernathsingh leaned back and graciously allowed his new acquaintance a chance to speak his mind.

"You hear me? *Like dog in this place.* If you not wearing a dog collar that say you belong to this firm, or working for this company, they does treat you worse: *like stray dog in this place.*"

It was close as Prash had ever come to revealing some private anguish. He stopped short, his voice cracking with sadness, of a full confession and he talked instead about people on welfare, about laziness, other forms of dog life he had observed among the people around him.

Jaggernathsingh sighed a huge sigh like a man whose burden it now was to explain the mysteries of America.

He said, "We Indians have a tradition of hard work. A lot of people from the estates coming up here now. Backdam people. You know what the problem in this country is? *Organisation*! We Indians not organised... Look at the Jews: they *organised*. Look at the Koreans: they *organised*. Italian people, they *organised*. We Indians have to stick together. We have to form some organisation... to render assistance to those in urgent need."

Prash sipped his beer and fell back into his listening pose.

Render assistance to those in urgent need. This was Jaggernathsingh, President of the Rice Marketing Board, speaking.

Despite what they thought about him back home, the man hadn't lost those qualities of speech-making that got his photo in the Republic's newspapers; and now up here he was full of big ideas.

For a while, his eyes locked in an attentive stare, Prash slipped into daydream. He was trying to see past the clothes, the newspaper words, the self-assurance of Jaggernathsingh; trying to imagine the domestic man – where did he live? Did he have his wife and children with him? He heard Jaggernathsingh say something about jobs:

"That's what organisation – they call it *networking* – could do... We need a president, a secretary, somebody who know computers... We could set up *contacts* to find jobs for people who just come up..."

Prash sat forward, leaning on his elbows; he wondered if he had missed something important on a matter close to his heart: jobs.

Jaggernathsingh, noticing his awakened interest, said, "I could fix you up with a job right now." He saw Prash fidget; he sensed his hesitation, his need; he pulled a pen from his pocket and scribbled a telephone number. "Tell them I send you," he said, not waiting for Prash to refuse or accept.

As soon as he could get to a telephone Prash called the number.

The young woman's voice on the line was terse and impatient; she put him on hold several times; when he mentioned Jaggernathsingh's name, Prash heard her telling someone in the office, "There's a guy here wanting to talk to Pauli, says he's a friend of Mick Jagger." Prash didn't like the way she giggled; on the line again the voice said she had a feeling the position had been filled; once more she put him on hold.

Just as he was about to hang up, a male voice asked him what he wanted. Slipping into his best American accent, Prash told the voice he'd worked before as an officer in his country's Defence Force. The voice on the line started listening. Prash spoke of weaponry and arrests, of one or two accidental deaths, of *the men under my supervision*.

He was told to come in for an interview.

At the interview, wearing dark glasses and a suit, he squared his shoulders and assured the man in a deep voice that he could take care of any business.

He was hired as a security guard.

The job came with a uniform and a night stick; Prash liked that; he also liked his hours, the night shift.

Round about ten o'clock he'd wander into the living room, adjusting his belt with the brass buckle, his body slapped with Brut cologne; he'd remind Sookmoon not to fill the Thermos to the brim with coffee; he was getting ready to leave his house at a dangerous hour, in terrible weather, for a job that was not without its hazards. He returned early the following morning swinging his night stick, and ignoring the drug-dealing riff-raff who hung about under shop awnings.

A few beers for breakfast, then he was off to sleep. He liked the idea of going to bed at the moment other people were preparing to go to work.

He shared the night shift with a man from the Dominican Republic, a short stocky fellow named Rodriggo Pizzarro. He had a round bald head, squinty eyes and the puffy bruised face of a former heavyweight contender. He was passionate about Dominican baseball players and Dominican women.

From him Prash learnt to use American idioms and to raise his voice a few decibel notches to just the right equalising pitch.

"Fucking prostitutes going crazy... they on drugs or something these days," Rodriggo Pizzarro would say.

"No shit!" Prash responded.

"I swear to God, they showing you everything, the whole

fucking warehouse spread out on the fucking sidewalk..."

"You gottabekidding!"

"*Mira*, yesterday morning, *right in front my building*, this woman see me coming up the block; she lift her skirt and bend over, showing me bare ass, *cleavage and bare ass*... spreading out the merchandise right there on the fucking sidewalk..."

"Getouttahere!" Prash laughed, for a story like this, no matter how sad or frightening, must be greeted with howling cynicism.

Then Rodriggo Pizzarro took the story into the realm of bizarre possibility.

"You know what she want?" he said. "Lemme tell you. She want someone to shove an umbrella up her ass, then open it! *That's* what she want."

Prash's laughter was one of genuine astonishment. To conceive an image as outrageous and grotesque as that! As violent and delightful as that! Only in America! For days and nights after, his mind, like a cat pawing a ball of wool, played with that delightful grotesquerie: shoving the umbrella up the woman's ass, then opening it.

His conversations with Sookmoon, restricted to sharp outbursts during the crossings their working hours allowed, now fell into a pattern of reproach and silence.

"Look, Man, don't give me stress," Sookmoon would say, after Prash complained she was coming home late, and her dinners were always the same, a bucket of Kentucky Fried Chicken. "I have enough problems with the subway, so don't start with me, *don't give me stress!*"

"*Problems with the subway!* Gimme a break, please! I got problems too, you know..." Prash would counter.

At some point Sookmoon fell silent as if paying more attention to her stress. This left Prash ignored and talking to himself:

"And where you going dress up like that... in socks and sneakers? Nobody does go to work in sneakers."

Sookmoon dressed in silence.

She was aware of his eyes watching her as she slipped into her clothes. She had changed her wardrobe, taking her cue from what she noticed other women wearing. Giving up the plain dresses of her village, she now wore sweaters with floral designs, and tightfitting pants which drew Prash's eyes to her bottom. (Once he asked her, "Is who you dressing up for?" She smiled and said nothing.) Her silence, the statement she was making with her body-fitting clothes, with her hair combed back showing more of her face, with touches of make-up, were daggers to his pride. He grumbled some more – "You and your flat bottom! You think anybody go turn to look at your flat bottom?" – and he made a big show of snuggling under the covers.

On the job things settled quickly into a routine, though soon enough Rodriggo Pizzarro found in Prash someone who spoke with a strange accent and had little to share from his day to day experience.

Prash told him he came from Pakistan, but when pressed he had little to say about Pakistani women.

Rodriggo Pizzarro brought in a portable television set, and showed off a new gold Rolex watch. Unable to compete manfully with purchases of his own, Prash started humming Hindi melodies like a man who had renounced the material world. Rodriggo Pizzarro began playing his transistor loud during their coffee break; it was tuned to a late-night Spanish station, the music fast, the words a thousand a minute. Prash sucked his teeth and wandered off a discreet distance to eat the sandwiches Sookmoon had prepared for him.

Slowly, inevitably, they lapsed into exchanging only the most obligatory of pleasantries.

The building he guarded was new, flat-roofed, some sort of paper factory that reminded him of the Industrial Park back in the Republic, a Government-run business venture active during the day, at night deserted. Prash couldn't imagine why anyone would want to break in; there was nothing worth stealing and selling as far as he could see; anyway it was easy work: clocking in, doing his time, clocking out.

It was here, at the start of Winter, sometimes dozing off, sometimes dreaming of his days at the wheel of his taxi, sometimes calculating how many months or years it would take on his current paycheck to save enough to return home set for life; it was here that he saw something he would not have seen anywhere else; something that caused subtle changes in his heartbeat, for it brought him close to the heartbeat of that other America.

The road outside the building he guarded was gravelly and tree-lined; it was therefore perfect for lovers. Prash heard the grinding of tyres on stones, saw the headlights extinguished, then the silence as in any bedroom of forbidden passion.

At first he couldn't understand why people needed to meet this way in America; he had always assumed there were motels as plentiful as McDonald outlets, built precisely for this purpose, for lovers who must conceal and satisfy their lust. In any case what could anyone really do in a parked car on a cold night, wearing sweaters and coats?

Sometimes on his way to work he passed a car or two locked tight and looking abandoned; the windows were often fogged up so he couldn't see the occupants. Not wanting to be taken for an intruder creeping up on cars parked on a lover's lane, he rolled up the collar of his jacket, bowed his head into the wind, and hurried forward as if there were some magnetic connection between himself and the building.

Now suddenly he started paying attention to what was happening on the road.

He did this out of a desire to distance himself from Rodriggo Pizzarro, his transistor, his long hours on the telephone (voice lowered, feet cocked up on a desk, an occasional lascivious laugh that deteriorated into an ugly-sounding cough); he did this out of boredom, out of an old habit of always looking outside at other people, anticipating drama of one kind or another.

It took him two nights of looking – or rather spying, since from his vantage point no one could see him – to determine there was a symmetry, a pattern to the meeting of lovers on this deserted road.

The cars arrived in twos; they parked one behind the other; the occupants came out – man and woman, man and man, woman and woman! They embraced; they re-entered one of the vehicles. Minutes later the vehicle shuddered as if its occupants, seatbelted again, were experiencing some metamorphosis, some form of transport out of this world; then the car was still, and Prash imagined that the lovers were indeed elsewhere, orbiting weightlessly in space.

Playful as this fantasy was, it made for deep anxieties Prash had about his marital life.

It loosened pleasanter thoughts: his wild days deflowering young girls in the canefields; his vagabond bachelor days in a community that expected from men a firm marriage and many children; days of rum-spiked ventures with women of other races in the city; days when he felt certain he had caught some untreatable disease; days of jokes and hysteria, as when for several months there was a shortage throughout the country of condoms due to a delayed shipment, or (some people were convinced) to socialist mismanagement of the economy.

In the end, as the lovers returned to their workaday bodies, started their cars and drove away, his thoughts came back to Sookmoon, their now barren (except for Sundays) bed.

One night he chanced to witness this:

Two cars drive up, shiny expensive models; the occupants alight and walk toward each other; (it had begun to snow, a fine dusting snow which would continue all night, transforming everything into a winter wonderland;) the man is long-haired and wears a long coat which makes him look tall and lean; the woman is demonstrably upset; mists of anger spurt from her mouth; she strikes him in the face; he stands rock-like, unimpressed; she falls on her knees and weeps at his feet; he turns to walk away, but is hindered by her arms, like leg irons around him. Calmly, he grasps her arms, drags her to her car, opens the door, bundles her in, slams the door; on an afterthought he opens the door, leans over, pulls down her pants, unbuttons his coats, and with the aplomb of a gunslinger fires his disgust into her exposed bottom, shot after shot, his body jerking from the pistol's kick; then he buttons his coat, bundles the woman back in the car, slams the door; stoops to pick up a shoe, opens the door to throw it in; slams it shut again, walking away like Jack Palance in *Shane*, his business done, the snow dusting his hair, his long coat.

Prash watched it happen, as on a screen, with silent fascination. He could do this only in America: watch two people kiss or stab each other (encounters so pure and private in their passion) and not feel involved.

But is none of your business! His heart raced, his blood rushed. Who were these people? *None of your business, Comrade!*

But how did the woman feel? What had gone on in the body of the man?

It didn't matter. These things happened in America. A big fish swallows a smaller fish even as the latter feasts between the thighs of tinier victims.

When he looked outside again the cars had gone. Hands in his pockets, he hummed a melody from the movie *Sholay*.

Filled with a new awareness, armed with bright new words – *who cares, fuck you, losers, it's a jungle out there, get a grip, sucker* – words he wasn't yet genuinely comfortable with, Prash now tried to erect the canopy of his America.

Life, he surmised, was beginning to look like this: you searched for your place of power, even as people tried to fuck over you; a place where you felt inviolable, at ease, as you primed and polished your pistol; while others, *the suckers out there*, walked the cold streets, told losers' angry tales, prayed and sang songs of freedom.

He thought of Sookmoon; he thought of the socialist republic back there, of Whappee and Errol back there; he thought of his taxi, the rum shop on the main road (six-pack beers were neat and challenging, but he missed the singing anarchy of rum); he thought of his forty-fifth birthday just passed; he didn't know what that number meant; he wished Whappee and Errol were here celebrate it with him.

He came to one conclusion about his life: at times it would spin and wobble out of his control. Whenever he felt certain he knew where he was going, something happened to tilt or wobble his world; he only knew what he felt and thought from day to day. The next morning, he might see something else, and there he'd go spinning again, scrambling again for control.

One afternoon, the sky as usual grey and deceptive, as he crossed a busy roadway, thinking he still had the green light, he found himself in the centre of the road, cars bearing down on him.

It was as if up to that moment he had been fast asleep; suddenly he awakened to car horns and exhaust pipes roaring like the fires of hell. He flailed his arms like a swirling red cape – *Na! Na! Na!* – and skipped out of the way; he stood on a traffic island, not completely out of danger, and he thought of his body, his gleaming black hair, his liquor-loving belly, his taxi driver's sure hands.

He thought: *All these bulls charging at me! I could get gored. I don't want to get gored in this country.*

10. Warp

Despite the ten years separating their lives, Sookmoon and Prash had this much in common: they grew up in a country described as developing, if you listened to the city socialists; or collapsing, if you believed the exaggerated tales of those who had packed up and fled.

Their community had lost its ancient power to shape their lives. Prash would whistle Hindi film melodies more out of nervous habit than any abiding faith. Sookmoon felt she was honouring her parents when she married the husband they had found for her.

As a young man, in a country where power supplies were erratic and youthful distractions limited, sexual conquest was the motor of Prash's life. He and his friends talked of little else – International Test Cricket, black market goods, *them socialist jackasses!* His taxi, his liquor, the young gals, the fellars – this was the sum of his life.

He had this fascination, too, with numbers; he kept scores the way cowboys in movies and comic books kept notches on their guns: how many women, how many times a week, how many conquests a year.

After his marriage to Sookmoon he gave up counting; he found out, with pain and surprise, that making love to his wife was more complicated than having sex with any woman; it was difficult and embarrassing to keep count; he found out, too, that his body was undergoing changes that made it frightening to keep count.

He tried several times to go back to his wolf-roaming ways, convinced that women still wanted it from him. To his chagrin he learnt that marriage had shut a door on his prowling past; the young girls liked it, yes; they did not want him anymore. His drinking habit increased and for a while he tried counting those ones for the road he took before going home to his marriage bed.

During those first years of married life it never occurred to Prash to share his private fears with Sookmoon. That was simply not his style. Whispering gentle words, kissing her, caressing her – that was not the way to happiness as a married man in the Republic.

As for Sookmoon, her first brush with men and their brute manhood happened at a wedding party, when she was sixteen: the ceremonies over, food and music and a pleasant drunkenness everywhere, swarms of thin old men and children, cousins and aunts: and an uncle who had flown in from Canada for the occasion: who kept looking at her from a distance, seeing in her pretty face hues of melancholy longing.

Late in the evening he was suddenly standing beside her, announcing he was going to the backdam to cut water coconuts: which was perfectly all right, except that he wanted company, Sookmoon's company, not the other screaming children; they were forbidden by her mother, even as Sookmoon was encouraged to go with her Uncle Basdeo.

They set off along a mud track behind the house, Sookmoon and her Uncle Basdeo; Sookmoon looking back once, catching her mother's eyes which held hers in sudden apprehension then abruptly turned away. And Sookmoon felt something, a churning sensation in her young woman's stomach, as if right at that moment in her life her mother had pushed her out to walk alone, to find her own way, in the fearful world of pestering young men.

And this troubled her as they moved deeper among the coconut trees, her uncle talking in his Canadian accent about the sweet life in Canada.

When they were far away from the wedding party, he stopped, dropped his machete, and whipped out a packet of condoms. "You know what this is?" he asked her, his eyes swollen and piercing behind bifocals.

Sookmoon didn't answer; she looked back through the foliage, searching again for her mother's eyes; her Uncle Basdeo's voice reminded her of schoolteachers with lust in their glances. He gripped her arms and pulled her down behind a tree; and although she resisted, she didn't struggle; she closed her eyes, smelling the liquor on his breath; she locked her thighs, listening curiously to his Canadian accent as he kept asking questions and fumbled with his zip.

As it turned out it was her uncle who struggled, who lost patience with her, getting mud on his Canadian-styled trousers; who never finished what, finally and desperately, he began, for they heard giggling sounds and they realised they'd been followed; they'd been *seen*.

He left her there, penetrated and in pain, embarrassed, her thighs sticky with amazing evidence, and in pain.

She didn't cry until she was completely alone; then she cried for her mother who let it happen; she cried because she knew it would happen again one day, even if she didn't want it to.

Those moments, left alone amidst the coconut palms, the music from the wedding party calling her back; that memory of humiliation in the backdam, she would carry inside her for the rest of her life.

For months after this incident she walked the village roads shamefaced, her head lowered, convinced that everyone *knew*, everyone was laughing at her.

She lived, too, in fearful fantasy: she had this notion that the erections of men remained stiff until their dogfaced in-out business was finished; she imagined that somewhere in Canada her uncle walked the streets concealing the bulge of an unsatisfied erection; she feared he would return one day to *her* body, tormented by the agony of his unfinished business, wanting release from that agony.

When the second occasion for intimacy approached, her mother was more reassuring. A husband had been found for her; instructions about marital duties were given; her mother presided over all the preparations and, teary-eyed, wished her long happiness.

When Prash climbed in bed beside her that first night, she found herself reacting as before with her Uncle Basdeo, her eyes shut tight, her thighs rigid, so that Prash had to force them apart, while she lay there watching him, smelling the liquor on his breath, telling herself all men were like her Uncle Basdeo, brutish, unsparing, dangerous if not allowed to finish their in-out business.

Later she began to notice differences in her man, weaknesses in Prash she thought she might use to her advantage.

For instance, Prash took rather too long, once he'd begun, to finish his business; if she screamed, it brought his performance to a quicker more satisfying end; if he came home drunk, he was inept and fell asleep the moment he was flat on his back; later he seemed more concerned with getting and keeping her pregnant.

Sookmoon learned secrets of control (of her body if not its fate) and manipulation; she cooked for Prash until he grew fat and lazy and gluttonous; she didn't ask too many questions when he came home late at night; after Ameena was born, she made visits to the city and kept a stock of contraceptive pills. This way she fed him bits and pieces of illusion that managed for the most part to keep his passions at bay.

But behind her silence, her dutiful manner, she herself was dreaming.

Her dreaming had started not with the Sears Catalogue Prash had found; it began that evening as she walked behind her Uncle Basdeo to the backdam, in those moments before his treacherous assault as he talked and talked in his Canadian accent about the sweetness of life in Canada.

11. The End's Beginnings

Christmas time in the city.

There were lights and Christmas trees and people jostling each other on the subway, gripping shopping bags and gift-wrapped packages.

Sookmoon and Prash were not seeing much of each other, and feeling less disposed to be merry. When their paths did cross in the evening their exchanges were more like the clash of stickfighters' shafts.

"You mean you home all morning, and couldn't take the clothes to the laundromat?" Sookmoon would protest. She had stumbled on the practical good sense of sharing domestic labour, after listening to the women she met at the laundromat who struck her as the loneliest, the most burdened women in the world.

"Wait! You expect me to come home from work, then go straight back to work, *washing clothes*? C'mon, gimme a break!"

"At least you could do some shopping at the supermarket. You leaving me to do all the work," she argued. It always seemed an untimely point to make, for right at that moment Prash was getting ready to go out in freezing temperatures to his job.

On Sunday mornings there was more time to talk. Sleeping off the accumulated weariness of the week, they woke up late, lay in bed under the comforter (Sookmoon did not object if he groped then muttered his desire for a little *sweetness*) and, depending on the postcoital mood, they brought each other up to date on the state of things.

"When last you look at your children? You know what problems Moolchand have?"

Prash waited to be told what problems Moolchand had.

It occurred to him he hadn't raised his hand to the boy for any reason in quite a while. And Sookmoon was right: he didn't know when last he'd looked at his children. The family didn't eat around a table that much; there were arbitrary comings and goings, people working odd hours. He was becoming a severely distracted man.

He walked the streets now, wary of attacks from idle people, crazy people, drug-injected people. He manoeuvred around them, never engaging their eyes. Gone, it seemed, were those days back home when, at the wheel of his taxi, he knew how to interpret the body language of people standing at the roadside, waiting for transport, or just liming.

One Sunday evening he decided to take a good look at Moolchand; the boy was eating dinner (this was the only time he appeared) in brooding silence, and getting ready to go back out. Rightaway Prash didn't approve of what he saw.

"So you cutting your hair like these black fellows," he said, hoping to draw him out contentiously. Moolchand said nothing.

"And how come, I don't see you in the daytime? You don't come home straight after school?" Moolchand made sounds of disgust through his teeth and got up from the table.

"Boy, I talking to you," Prash shouted. Something was happening here that seemed a bypass of, if not a challenge to, his authority.

He found out from Sookmoon that Moolchand had been intercepting letters from the school inviting his parents to a conference.

"They say he not going to school. He hanging about outside with some street boys. They give him two report cards, and he tear them up. They put him in Special Ed. Is a class for handicapped children."

"*Handicapped* children? You put this boy in a school for *handicapped* children?"

"Why you don't go talk to the teachers? You home all day doing nothing. Why *you* don't go to their *conference*?"

Prash had never used that word before. He felt intimidated by it; he had no idea what happened at conferences. He was also wary of the prospect of having to explain his son's truancy, and at the same time demand an explanation for Moolchand's handicapped status. Besides, the teachers were bound to ask him questions, all sorts of questions.

All this was damn foolishness! *Conference*, my backside! There was only one way to settle it.

The following evening when Moolchand showed up and was midway through dinner at the table, Prash emerged from the bedroom, half-dressed (the hardworking father who must spare a moment to resolve a crisis in the family). With a broad belt in his hand he delivered the first blow to the back of Moolchand's head. He savoured the shock and surprise on Moolchand's face. Then he declared:

"So you's a big man now! Walking away from me when I talking to you..."

His intention was to give the boy a good beating, making up for months of perceived neglect. The result was tumultuous: smashed plates, spilled food, overturned chairs, the table cloth sliding to the floor, as Moolchand tried half-successfully to get out of the way. Sookmoon was screaming with alarm.

Moolchand rushed to the doorway, turned, examined the welts on his arm, then uttered what would be his last spoken words to his father: "You old shit you! Hit me again! You hit me again, and I call the police on your rass!" With that he made his escape, slamming the door.

There was a hiatus, a break in the storm, during which Prash stood feeling not quite finished, and not quite sure about that reference to the police. Right at that moment Ameena walked in.

Her appearance gave Prash the pretext to empty himself of his residual rage.

"And where *you* been all this time?" he asked her. She looked up, stunned and frightened, her face still raw from the icy air outside. "You *going* to the same school; you *know* you brother hanging outside with street boys; you don't say *nothing*? You covering up for him, *eh, eh*?"

He hit her twice across the face; she whimpered and folded herself against his fury; he might have hit her again, had not Sookmoon grabbed him by the arm, her wailing now sirens of great distress.

When it was over, silence like a gentle mist spread through the apartment. To Prash in the bathroom, applying skin lotion and Brut cologne to his body, head slanted as he combed his hair, it was the silence of respect, of old habits and expectations restored. When Sookmoon came inside later her anger was muted, her manner appeasing.

"You didn't have to hit 'Meena. She doing good in her class. Is not her fault... They could call the police on you for hitting these children... they have laws in this country... is not like back home... you could go to jail for child abuse in this country."

He wasn't listening to her. A new feeling was coursing through his body in the wake of his rage. Something inside him, beast or spirit, had come alive. He couldn't put a name to it; he didn't stop to reflect on its source; he knew it was inside him like hot lava boiling and roaring in his belly.

When he left the apartment it was there, in his padded shoulders and arms, in his sailor's gait as if the sidewalk were a roiling sea. He was now a force to be reckoned with, inspiring fear like Spencer Tracy in *Bad Day At Black Rock*; people, it seemed, were moving out of his way as he hurried to the bus stop; his jaws moved up and down, assiduously chewing gum (the gum lost its sugary taste too quickly, he felt like a cud-chewing cow, but he didn't mind): he was walking like a man more to be feared than knowing fear.

When he came in on Rodriggo Pizzarro that night, his greeting was louder and heartier than usual, more American! Throbbing with new confidence, he was ready to engage in the kind of anecdotal exchanges Rodriggo Pizzarro enjoyed.

"This woman on the train," he began, removing his jacket "...was sitting next to this guy... quiet, quiet... not saying a word. When the train pull in, she get up... and slap him... BAM... just like that, right 'cross his face... then she walk out... quiet, quiet..."

Rodriggo Pizzarro, looking impressed and bemused, turned down his transistor radio.

Prash felt encouraged to recount the episode with embellishments of time, location, what the lady looked like. They spent most of the night in this spirit of camaraderie, swapping stories about weak men and stupid women, *los patos* or *auntiemen*, about people who found themselves *in the wrong place at the wrong time*, or who *didn't give a fuck!*

Prash took a bold step later that same night, leaving his job two hours early – "No problem. I take care of everything," Rodriggo Pizzarro assured him – and rushing home, scaring the daylights out of Sookmoon when he entered the bedroom at that strange morning hour, announcing his intention, his unstoppable need, to make love to her right that minute, before she got ready to go to work.

Once he had recovered some semblance of power in his home, Prash withdrew into a tower of forbidding silence from which he occasionally grunted or signalled his wishes with the minimum of words. Sookmoon fell back into her old secondary role; she found that talking to him was like a weary climb up a stairway to a sullen tower. Still, on Sunday mornings, or whenever she could, she spoke to him about the city and her job and their still unclear plans for the future.

The lady in Manhattan, whose child and home she cared for and cleaned, gave her cause for much comment. "She always talking loud, even when I standing next to her... she have bad breath and bad nerves. She taking all kinds of pills, you should see how many bottles of pills she have in the medicine cabinet."

Prash grunted.

"What happening now? You and the lady stop *clicking*?" he asked in an acid tone.

Happy to have roused his attention, Sookmoon rushed on:

"She does spoil the little boy... let him do whatever he want, then calling me to clean up the mess... saying to him, *Christopher, you really shouldn't do that!*"

Prash made sniggering sounds.

"Then the other night, like her sweet man sleep over. The next morning I find his *thing*, the condom he use, knot up and lying on the floor by the bed. Like he forget to pick it up. I just leave it right there. She come telling me the next day how I not cleaning the room properly. I knew what she was talking about, but I refuse to touch it, no way!"

Prash snorted with contempt.

"Come telling me I must do a proper job or else! She know she can't get nobody else to dress up in sari and serve roti and curry when she invite her friends..."

This frozen state of relations ended abruptly the day Prash lost his second job.

Rodriggo Pizzarro waited until he was about to clock out one morning, then he broke the news. "Sorry, *amigo*, but that's how it is. The company laying off people. It's a cruel world, *papi*."

This rupture came at a time when he felt his friendship with Rodriggo Pizzarro had been sealed; they were *amigos*, buddies; it was, therefore, a shattering blow; he was angered that the man had not put up a fight to protect him, had let him go with a hard smile, and a simple *that's how it is*.

He explained all this to Sookmoon, coming down from his tower and breaking his silence. His voice swung between frustration and a whining lament.

"In this place, you can't trust nobody. Your own friend could stab you in the back. *Like Brutus, a butcher knife in your back!*"

A week later, on an impulse, he left the house late one night, intending to drop in casually on Rodriggo Pizzarro. The streets somehow seemed more dangerous now that he wasn't purposefully on his way to work. When he got there his suspicions were confirmed.

There was someone else on the job, a new face in the security guard uniform; Rodriggo Pizzarro looked surprised to see him, and said something in Spanish to the new man who slunk away.

There were uncomfortable moments. Prash didn't know what to say. His voice was a clarinet of anguish, his responses slow and curt. He was flooded with anger but he didn't know how to be angry with Rodriggo Pizzarro. Besides, he didn't speak Spanish and (it occurred to him right then) he hadn't really known Rodriggo Pizzarro that long.

Abruptly, feeling like a fool for assuming so much, he left the building.

"In this country, everybody looking out for their own kind," he announced to Sookmoon. "Is a *true true* thing! The Jews looking out for the Jews, the Mafia for the Mafia people, the Spanish for the Spanish..."

"Maybe we should move to Queens. I hear more o' we people living there," she said.

"If I moving anywhere, is home I going. As a matter of fact, I think is time we move back."

Sookmoon sensed the tide turning once again; she braced herself, reined in her impulse to soothe his nerves.

She said not one word more.

Back on his own time, feeling strangely happy not to be working those awkward late hours, Prash pondered his next move.

He rode the subway during off peak hours, studying the faces on the train; he wondered if all the people he saw waiting for trains or walking the streets were also jobless, adrift, all dreaming they'd be tapped on the shoulder one day by soft fingers of the dream.

One morning he thought of surprising Sookmoon in the park where she took the white lady's boy for a stroll; he discovered that the sidewalks of Manhattan played tricks with his sense of direction. You turn a corner, thinking you're going East; you end up bewildered by the stone, glass and towering buildings, jostled by the crowds, a victim for lurking sharp-eyed muggers.

He tried searching for his own kind, those backdam people who had fled the Republic. He discovered many who looked like them; he tried to catch their eyes; they looked away or ignored him, distrusting his unsolicited glance.

Where did they all go – the backdam people who had left everything behind, lock, stock and barrel for America?

On the train one afternoon he thought he found one of them: a dark-skinned round-eyed girl whose roots, he felt sure, went all the way back to the sugar estates in the Republic. She had boarded the train with her friends, all on their way home from school, but she sat alone, her arms crossed, her eyes staring up at the roof of the train. Shy, isolated, a little frightened – perhaps she'd recently come up.

The train stopped; two of her friends, changing seats, flopped down beside her and asked what she did last weekend. "I went to Coney Island," the girl said, in a firm American accent. Her friends looked taken aback. "Coney Island!" she repeated. "What do you people do in New York?"

That was the end of his search! The end, too, of his time here in America! Going back home to the Republic, he decided, was the right move to make!

The old life was waiting for him, unchanged: the village, the rumshop on the main road, his taxi, cinders of canetrash in the air (though now he really liked the flurries of falling snow): the safe harbour, familiar routines.

From the streets of this city the Republic seemed a blemished paradise; a troubled weary place, yes; but not a hungry place; not war-torn like other countries he had heard about.

The battery in the taxi was probably dead by now. He could take back a brand new dependable American-made battery. He could ship back *a whole car*, a second-hand American-made car with spare parts packed in the trunk! He could, after all, move back, take up where he'd left off, even if he hadn't been to Coney Island.

"Home is home, Comrade," he said to himself, throwing those words around his shoulders like a strong arm of comfort and conviction.

On New Year's Eve, a day that threatened to rain bitterly, washing out whatever people planned on doing at midnight, he felt the need for fellowship, for conversation and good cheer; he went in search of Jaggernathsingh.

He couldn't find him anywhere inside his favourite restaurant. Just as he turned to leave, one of the waitresses said, "If you looking for Mr Jaggers he's in his office."

His office? Mr Jaggers?

Prash knocked on the door; he heard a muffled voice say imperiously, "Come!"

Jaggernathsingh was on the telephone; he waved Prash in, and continued talking; or rather listening, responding in affirmatives, his brow knitted in concentration, so that Prash was left to figure out this latest in remarkable transformations: from the man he'd first met sitting dolefully on a bench pock-marked with bird droppings, to this new man at his desk with the pen holder, in his office.

He caught himself looking enviously around the office. Scowling, he came to a swift conclusion: this Jaggernathsingh in his three-piece suit, doing amazing escapist tricks like Houdini; this Jaggernathsingh calling himself Mr Jaggers was nothing but a thief, a liar, a runaway, a disgrace to his nation.

Jaggernathsingh put down the phone, got up, extended his hand and said, "How you doing, Comrade?"

Prash shook hands limply, and said, "Happy New Year!"

"Oh yes," Jaggernathsingh said, happy to be reminded of the day's significance. "This calls for a little celebration."

From a drawer in his desk he pulled out a bottle of rum from the Republic. "Check this out, Comrade. Come in only last week. Friend of mine went home and I tell him don't forget to bring back a bottle of *ten-year*. We could fire one right now."

Prash stared at his beloved amber; he felt more homesick than ever; he relaxed and tried to put out of his mind his image of Jaggernathsingh as a disgrace to his nation. His head was a beehive of resentment, flashing images, blunt questions he wanted to ask Jaggernathsingh.

When the waitress came in with glasses on a tray, smiling at her boss, Prash felt his anxieties fading away.

He poured his rum and told himself: *you sitting in the man's office; you drinking his rum; is New Year's Eve, forget all that nonsense, man!*

Easier said. No sooner had they clinked glasses, ringing in the New Year, than Jaggernathsingh asked, "So what's happening, Comrade?"

Prash felt cornered.

Nothing was happening in his life. There was the old anxiety about job loss (he didn't want Jaggernathsingh to think he had come to be rescued by another telephone number). There was the old fear about his real purpose here in America. Compared with Jaggernathsingh, he seemed unable to get his act together.

"I going home, Comrade," he announced with ignited confidence, slouching in the chair.

Jaggernathsingh sat back, feigning surprise and interest. "Well, the Comrade Leader used to say, *All History is the movement of peoples*."

"This was only a long holiday for me," Prash heard himself say. "I just come up to make a few Yankee dollars, do some shopping, pick up spare parts for the car. Now I going back home." After he had said all that he felt a lift in his spirits.

Jaggernathsingh smiled and nodded; he was waiting to hear more.

Prash got the feeling as he reached for ice cubes that Jaggernathsingh – his mind a shopkeeper's scales – was now taking stock of their separate fortunes: calculating how far each man had moved up in this world from their roots in the village: comparing the decisions each man had made to shape his destiny. And here was Prash announcing his next move, his latest decision: going back home.

"Yes, man, the wife complaining all the time 'bout the cold weather, and how she miss home," he said.

And since a smug smile still glowed on Jaggernathsingh's clean-shaven businessman's face, Prash veered away from what might have been a precipitous tumble into more deceit and lies. He said, "So, you's some big shot in this place, man!"

Jaggernathsingh sighed another of his weary, pained sighs, as if shifting some unseen burden from one shoulder to the other.

He ignored the nudge toward self-revelation. He encouraged Prash to freshen his drink, and steered the conversation toward the durable sensations of ten-year old rum. Then, out of the blue: "I planning a big move myself. I going home too, Comrade."

It was Prash's turn to feign amazement, to wait for Jaggernathsingh to go on.

Instead Jaggernathsingh stalled, opening a gold cigarette case; offering Prash a cigarette, lighting up, exhaling – all of this in a deliberate manner that seemed to set the stage for his next expanded statement.

"Seriously Comrade, I planning something that never happen in our country before... a *movement* to get rid of them bandits running the Government." (Jaggernathsingh drawing on his cigarette; Prash waiting to burst out laughing, for it was still Christmas Eve, and this had to be a story with a funny ending). "This is serious, Comrade... is revolution we talking 'bout..." (Laugher oozing up to Prash's face, making it ripe and shiny.) "Fellows in Toronto organising the whole thing... We have *contacts* already in the Republic... in the Defence Force... I telling you this, 'cause when the time come to move, we going need people like you to mobilise support."

"*People like me!*" Prash made his laughter sound a little self-deprecating.

Jaggernathsingh leaned back and joined in the unintended humour. He raised his glass and offered a toast to changes in the Republic. He looked at the bottle appreciatively and said:

"I hear the Comrade Leader does drink only imported Scotch. *Johnny Walker*! Well, he could keep that. *This* is grassroots stuff, the choice of the people!"

Prash agreed. Feelings of grassroots homesickness welled up inside him.

"So when you leaving," Jaggernathsingh asked.

"I aint fix the date yet. I got to make reservations..."

"Listen," Jaggernathsingh's voice dropped back down to its conspiratorial level. "I want you to take back something for me... Don't worry. I have contacts at the airport. Tell me when you flying; give me your flight number, and we'll fix everything... You shipping back a barrel?"

Prash said he was thinking of buying a car and shipping that back for resale.

"No problem. T*he deal is clean*! I have *contacts* at Customs. Chap from the West Bank, Jay Jainarine... *Jai Jai*... you know him? You could send back anything you want. As a matter of fact, we could work out something whereby we shipping stuff from Stateside in your name... and you picking it up... not to worry, *the deal is clean*. My contacts will fix everything... we have people in high places... ready to move as soon as we give the signal..."

The telephone rang; Jaggernathsingh answered, listened; knitted his brow, once again the businessman in his office; Prash felt it was time to go.

He didn't like sitting around while Jaggernathsingh was on the phone. Besides, his spirit though leavened by alcohol was not exactly at peace with the world.

He plunged out into the cold, where people hurried by and the sky seemed determined to unleash turbulence for the New Year; and everyone carried his head on his shoulders like a basket filled with longings and perishable dreams; no one knew about the astonishments of good ten-year rum; and no one really cared if a government was murdering its people in a republic somewhere.

He kept thinking about Jaggernathsingh with his new fancy words: *the deal is clean*.

Amazing how some people in their journey through this world could invent for themselves new lives: over and over, ruthlessly, single-mindedly, a new life.

Take this Jaggernathsingh, this amazing Jaggernathsingh: born and schooled like Prash in a village back in the Republic; here he was, after various transitions, talking of revolution and his *contacts*; not a word about the money he embezzle from the Rice Marketing Board; living like some Brahmin in New York, untouched by anyone; *a man who dreamed big movements.*

While he, Prash, had known only his world of small petty runnings, his furtive pleasures: a mean life all through which he had yearned for one sparkling diamond from time, one astounding decisive act (no, not his marriage to Sookmoon, not coming to America) that would transform him, that would lift him out of nobodiness.

And now it seemed Jaggernathsingh was pushing that diamond towards his hands, was suggesting his moment was near.

All he had to do when he returned home was to become a contact, await some signal from Toronto; receive shipments, and dispense goods from Stateside; it could make him an important man, if he played it smart.

And I could play smart. I know to play better than any pandit, businessman or priest. I could spin ball or tale better than any o' them.

Maybe... but wait, is power you playing with there now... raw power and grave risk... and suppose... and besides... and you never could tell...

"You listening? Moolchand drop out of school. He get a job and he making good money," Sookmoon was saying a little fearfully.

He turned on his side in the bed, as immovable by her words as boulders by water.

She reminded him the rent was due soon again; that they had to decide once and for all how long they would stay in America.

He heard her, but paid little attention.

Angered by his indifference, she burst out once more, "Is what wrong with you and this Lysol disinfectant? You spraying it all over the bathroom like if is perfume! Smelling up the whole house! You have a problem?"

"Joke! Big joke! You shoulda marry Jerry Lewis and raise a whole pack o' jokers!" Prash replied.

"They looking for a new security guard in a building on the Grand Concourse," Sookmoon said.

He turned on his back, sucked his teeth and muttered to himself, "That Jaggernathsingh..."

"They want a man with *experience*. Now you have *experience*. You could tell them where you been working before," she said.

She knew Prash very well; she need only leave the information to warm over in his head like late dinner in an oven.

"That Jaggernathsingh," Prash said again, scratching his groin, "you know, I wonder what happen to his wife and children."

12. Jaws & Clyde "The Slide"

"But wait, how you hear 'bout this job?"

"You talk to the people? You get it?"

"And what happen to the fellow who use to work there?"

"Somebody push him off the roof of the building."

He had already secured the job; he'd had no problem persuading the Super that despite his strange accent he was *experienced*, and didn't use drugs, and could produce papers to prove his residency status. He hadn't thought of asking about the man he was replacing; and now here was Sookmoon saying *somebody push him off the roof of the building*, speaking of an act of cold-blooded murder in the same nonchalant way she had sent him straight towards the scene of that most recent crime.

Actually, Sookmoon and Ameena spent hours at the dining table recounting the day's horrors. Prash considered it women's gossip and kept aloof: a newborn baby thrown down the incinerator, a young woman raped on the subway ("and everybody just move to the next carriage"), Spanish-speaking women putting up with a lot of slackness from Spanish-speaking men. Sookmoon and Ameena talked as if all this was America, and what could they do about it – Ameena carried a pocket knife in her purse – except *don't take no shit from nobody*.

The following day Prash walked around the site of his new job like a building inspector. He kept craning his neck, looking up, staring at the walls: hard, bare, unspeaking walls.

There was no one on the roof at the time. The walls looked just as the builders had intended them to look: brick walls with fire escape steps and, here and there, air-conditioning units propped on the sills of the windows; functional bare walls, in need of fresh coats of paint, that kept out the cold; the kind of wall that would delight only those squirrels he used to watch scurrying and climbing and amusing themselves.

Somebody push him off the roof. Just like that!

He wondered if the man had put up a struggle, if he'd held on to the rim of the roof, screaming for his life; if anyone could have heard him behind these walls; if he had screamed as he plummeted past the shaded windows; if his head or his legs hit the ground first; and how much the snow might have softened the fall.

Something about death and violence in this country alarmed him, kept him perplexed all that day. This sort of thing happened. Every day in America. A cold private act. The body discovered with shock and lingering horror. An act as casual as farting. *Off the roof of the building.*

Prash was stationed in the lobby of the building, its floors waxed shiny, almost slippery underfoot if you weren't careful.

His job was to deter any *strange-looking people* from entering unchallenged. There was a chair, a table and a visitor's book in which the name and time of any visitor's arrival was noted. It seemed on the surface an uncomplicated task.

He wore the uniform from his old job, the serge pants and the blue shirt; he sported a beige state trooper's hat he'd bought from a skinny man who talked fast and asked for five bucks; he thought his uniformed presence would deter disagreeable people, and go a long way towards winning the cooperation of everyone, resident and visitor alike.

Very quickly he learnt the patterns of movement in the building.

Early in the morning he stood with his hands behind his back and watched the departure of working mothers, children off to school, all brisk and fresh-faced. He smiled and said *Have a good day!* to anyone who caught his eye.

A few hours later there was a stirring in the lobby as welfare mothers and the retired came down to clear their mailboxes. The maintenance crew, keys jangling from chains on their left and right hips, made jokes as they headed to the elevators. In the afternoon, the children returned, holding the doors open too long, careless with their clothes, their bags, careless with each other.

Relaxed, Prash sat at his desk and read a newspaper; he opened the door for old ladies fumbling with their keys; *strange-looking people* were rare; visitors, impressed by his formal demeanour, seemed willing to cooperate.

Whenever he saw the Super he said, "What's happening, Skipper?" and assured him, "Everything under control".

Sometimes, when he felt like stretching his legs a little, he took the elevator to the top floor, then walked back down the stairs to the lobby. Glancing up and down the empty corridors – checking for strange customers – he wondered what life was like for each resident behind the closed doors.

Sometimes fragments of conversation as people walked by inflamed his curiosity: *he beat the shit out of her*, someone would say, making Prash wonder how *he* did it; or, *those bitches just making babies*.

On occasion he stopped in the hallway and listened for tell-tale sounds. Not a whimper came from behind those doors.

Sometimes the muffled pounding of a stereo, or a television running; otherwise not a clue about people's lives, what they said to each other, how they hated or loved, their obsessions, their jokes, how they survived alone.

The trouble (for which he imagined himself always ready, though he had no idea in what shape or form it would test him) began with the school children: noisy, jostling, downright un-disciplined kids who left in the morning with their harried mothers, who returned on their own, their jackets grimy, hold-ing the door open too long, letting in draughts; and *shouting*, always shouting, in the lobby; so that Prash was sometimes compelled to bellow, "Stop this blasted noise!" when their shouting reached intolerable levels.

They'd lower their voices until they got to the elevators; they'd sneer, "You're not my father!" as they walked away; they'd laugh and say derisory things in Spanish.

"They does let these children run *wild wild* all 'bout this place," he said to Sookmoon.

She agreed and lamented the general lack of manners; she told him again about Christopher in Manhattan, how his mother was spoiling the child. (When they were left alone, she said, she tried to teach Christopher *manners*).

One day this kid with silver braces on his teeth – his friends called him Jaws – who kept running in and out of the building took offence when Prash threatened to tell his mother. He disappeared up the stairs, then returned with two of his friends, the peaks of their hats pointing backward; and he waved a pistol under Prash's nose.

"Mess with me, and I'll pop you!" he declared, his words bouncing like swatted tennis balls off the lobby walls.

Undeterred by the threat – he refused to believe the pistol was real – Prash stopped the boy's mother the following morning, and complained to her about his attitude.

"This boy here have no respect for nobody. Every day he coming in, making one set o' noise in the place. *No manners, no respect!*"

To his amazement the boy fired back on the spot, denouncing Prash as a liar and interrupting him with loud disavowals; he told his mother Prash had threatened to hit him, had threatened to hit other children.

The woman, at first bewildered, then irritated at being delayed, seized on this last fabrication and warned Prash against *striking any child in this building*.

Right at that point – as people stopped, hearing raised voices, and looked at Prash, wondering what was going on – it occurred to Prash that the pistol waved in his face the day before might have been, indeed, a loaded death-dealing weapon.

"They growing up like criminals," he remarked to Sookmoon that night. "Barefaced liars and criminals."

She wasn't sure whom he was referring to, but she mentioned in the next breath that Ameena had been a victim of choke-and-rob.

Prash was stunned. He came out of the bathroom, shaving cream lathered on his face, his mouth open in disbelief.

"Right in front the school. This man walk up behind her and snatch the chain from her neck. *A good good gold chain*, not that washed out gold they wearing here. 'Meena was so shocked! She couldn't see his face, he had the hood from the jacket over his head."

"You mean, this girl get robbed and is only now you telling me 'bout it?"

"Look, don't give me stress! You not interested in these children. Besides, what you could do about it now? The chain gone already."

Prash's face seemed to swell in consternation; he summoned Ameena from her room and demanded a full account of what had happened. She lowered her head; she told him she'd forgotten all about it; there was no point in going over details.

Prash flew into a rage; Ameena retreated to her room; Sookmoon accused him again of neglecting the children, of leaving everything in her hands.

"Is time we move out of this area," she said.

Prash dropped the argument like a brick and went back to the bathroom. He puffed his cheeks and moved the razor with deliberate care; he studied the line of his sideburns and moustache, all the while thinking about the new cracks that had appeared in his world.

The following day in the lobby the children couldn't fail to notice a different Prash. He wore the state trooper's hat, a pair of sunglasses and he carried a night stick hooked to his waist. He stood silent and menacing, like Clint Eastwood in *A Fistful of Dollars*, coolly chewing gum, as if armed and ready to take on all noise-makers.

Jaws and his friends went in and out, making pistol gestures with their fingers and saying *Boom!* (It sounded like *booosh*, a convincing imitation, the hand jerking back with the recoil). But now they were puzzled by his lack of reaction, by the way he just stood there on one foot, hands folded, *staring*.

Prash himself didn't know what he was about. Of one thing he was certain: this place was now a war zone. Ameena had been touched by one of these criminals. Somewhere out there someone was wearing a gold chain brought all the way from the Republic, *good good gold*, as Sookmoon had said. He was keeping his eyes peeled just in case that someone walked by.

He had no idea what he would do in the event of a real show-down. Still, he wasn't going to allow himself to be scared by pistols or threats or gold chain thieves. Standing there, watchful and menacing, was for the time being his statement to anyone out there.

"Let them play with me!" he muttered to himself. When the lobby was empty he started pacing the floor.

"Let them try any shit with me!" he said, louder this time. Then he began whistling songs from the movie *Sholay*.

Days went by. He discovered that life had a way of loosening up stiff joints caused by ephemeral hurts. Rising always to new mornings of hope and possibility, people simply forgot or paid no more attention to the nightmares of yesterday. Even Jaws' mother, in a cheerier mood one day, smiled and said, "How you doing?"

Lowering his guard a little, Prash began to feel that his role and person had at last been accepted. He smiled a bit more, learning now to *wear* the smile, putting it away when it wasn't needed.

He was sitting one morning, reading the newspaper (paying close attention now to reports of crime; noticing how frequently and with what frightening consequences they occurred in the Bronx) when he heard someone shaking the door. A fellow in a trench coat, carrying a paper bag. Signalling furiously that he wanted to be let in. *A strange looking person!*

Prash hesitated; he hitched up his pants and took his cool time walking to the door. The fellow brushed right past him.

"Hold on there, fellow... Excuse me, you have to sign your name in this book," Prash said, not liking this fellow one bit.

"I live in this building. Who the *fuck* you think you are?"

"Look here, guy, you have to sign..."

"Fuck you!" the man spat, walking away, his mouth twisted in fury as he hurled at Prash more *fuckyous*.

It sounded like a shoot-out in the building lobby, the man's words like so much rifle fire reverberating in a canyon.

Fuck you! Never before had Prash felt so wounded and thrown back, so impacted. ("These black fellows have lungs like cannons," he'd said to Sookmoon once. "They don't talk like normal people. They does *fire* words at you.")

Now, he realised, he'd come face to face with people in a way he wasn't yet prepared for: people whose anxieties hung like grenades on their chests. Touch them, pull the pin by mistake, and emotions went off. *Fuck you!* They stared at you as if they were taking aim. *Fuck you!* They pointed arms and long fingers like rifles.

It left his body feeling riddled, with lacerations tearing his bowels; and though he wanted to get even right on the spot, to take back the power he felt he'd momentarily lost in the exchange, he hadn't yet mastered the reflexes, the quick verbal draw to fire back. He returned to his desk and sat there brooding.

A sour nauseous feeling once more rose and fell in his stomach. He had railed at Sookmoon about this *bad feeling*, blaming her for not cooking enough of his favourite foods. He might have to knock some sense into her, make her stop this nonsense.

He heard footsteps and voices and he looked up. Two fellows were on their way out. Wearing black trench coats.

One of them was the fellow who had just brushed past. He pointed a long finger at Prash: "Muddahfucker there was trying to slow me down!"

The two men hesitated at the door. Prash sensed that this was the showdown.

One of them – short, stocky, sporting a goatee and a gold-capped tooth – sauntered over to him.

Prash shifted his body, braced himself.

"Howyadoing, my man?" The man was smiling. His voice was a singing falsetto, full of brotherly affection, intending no harm. "I hear you're having problems with my man here." Sitting now on the edge of Prash's desk, giving off a powerful cologne; *my man here* slack-hipped and glowering at the door.

Prash standing up: "You live here, right? Well, you see, we have *procedures* in this building." Sounding like Jaggernathsingh, President of the Rice Marketing Board: "You see, anybody who don't live in this building must sign in this book when they comes through that door."

Singing falsetto, a little puzzled by the accent, but nodding as if he understood perfectly well: "You only doing your job, I hear you." Prash folding his arms, nodding too. "Man has got to make a living like anybody else." The fellow at the door, muttering, still glowering. "And that's cool... but see here, my man... this brother now lives in this building, unnerstand? I mean, HE LIVES IN THIS BUILDING, *unnerstand?*" Opening the trenchcoat so that Prash could see clearly the gun tucked in his waistband.

And Prash fidgeted. This was the second time a gun had been displayed before him. He stood his ground and held his stare behind sunglasses.

Fellow at the door, swearing, wanting to go. "Hey, I'm talking to my man here. You go ahead, I'll be with you in a second." Turning again to Prash, extending his hand, "My name is McBride. *Clyde 'The Slide' McBride*. What you say your name was?"

Prash took the hand, matching the firm grip, sensing somehow he was being drawn away from where he felt more secure.

"Where you from?" singing falsetto asked. Prash told him India.

"India... *riiiight!* I know this brother, he from India too! Got that newspaper stand? Near 170th & Jerome? See, I understand where you're coming from. It's like you're here now, in the U.S.A., cause *the man* in India won't let you *be*... won't let you make a living... but, see, *the man* here's doing the same thing. Been doing the same thing to the brothers for years. Trying to keep us *down*, make us stay on the reservation, *unnerstand*, when all we want is to make a living."

Singing falsetto shaking his body and pumping himself up with laughter, for he feels he has scored a huge point.

Prash watched him.

"See... is the same shit *wherever* the man is in control. And you and me, we want the same thing, *right?* Aint nobody going to keep us on the reservation if we don't want to stay there, *right?*"

And Prash at a loss for words: alarmed, since never before had anyone spoken to him this way. Face grim, lips tight, nodding, waiting. Not wanting to appear stupid and uncomprehending. Knowing the fellow would eventually shut up and go away; knowing, too, it would be smart to stay on the friendly side of this man with his trench coat, his pistol, his sullen friend, and that singing falsetto.

"So what I'm saying is this: I'm taking care of business, you're taking care of business. Same thing I told the other guy who was here – the one who had the little accident on the roof? – but, see, he didn't dig the groove... we had a little *miscommunication*! So here's what I'm saying, my man: from time to time the brothers will come calling... strictly business, *unnerstand*... but we don't want problems, *unnerstand*, we don't need no hassle."

Standing erect now, buttoning up his trench coat, smiling, so that Prash, not knowing why, smiled back.

"There could be a little something in this for you if you're smart, know what I'm saying?"

Prash not sure, but nodding now and slapping the man's outstretched palms the way he'd seen it done in the streets.

"I hear you," Prash said finally in a firm new voice.

"*Arrrright!*... my man hears me! ...Oh one more thing." At the door, his long fingers making magic in the air. "Why you so hard on the kids? ...Lighten up, my brother. They got to make a living too, *unnerstand*?" Winking. Hurrying away. Catlike on his feet.

And right then, as the profile of the man moved through the glass doors, it touched Prash with its lightning rod. The feeling he had had of being menaced faded. It was replaced with a sense of wonder, with a village boy's longing for global romance and adventure as he trudged home on dark country roads after a late night cinema show.

Prash walked to the door and watched as the two men, singing falsetto and his sullen sidekick, stood on either side of a shiny red car, their hands on the door handles. They looked up the road, hatless cowboys studying specks on the horizon, then they climbed in almost simultaneously.

He wondered where they were going. A couple of blocks? Downtown? Across the state line?

Light on their feet. Belonging to no one and no place. Not the Republic. Not the reservation. Not *the man*.

When Sookmoon came home that evening she found him in an excited voluble mood. She dropped her bags and hurried into the bathroom. He couldn't wait for her to come out. He shouted through the door, telling her he'd reached a decision about their lives. Not a word about his encounter with the two men in trench coats. "I know what we going to do now," he told her.

Waiting for him to go on, Sookmoon smiled behind the bathroom door, like a woman who had borne his children and had known him from the day he had climbed into her bed. She felt as if something stressful had ended at last.

13. Leche

In the days that followed Prash felt the enormous relief of a man who had pushed a boulder up a steep hill all his life, sweating and heaving every day, always wondering how much more he had to go; choosing one morning to let it go; in one blinding stroke abandoning both boulder and hill; walking away from the futility of that task; marvelling at how easy it was to walk away.

He'd found a new freedom of mind and arms and limbs, as if there were now fixtures of bird wings to his body. And though he might have had difficulty explaining himself to anyone back in the Republic, here in America Prash was certain he had become a new man.

In the lobby he now seemed a more quixotic person, at times engaging, smiling and joking with everyone, at other times self-absorbed or even sullen.

When the kids came storming in after school he ignored their shouting, or simply disappeared from his desk. He discarded the state trooper's hat and sunglasses; he no longer cared for the image of feared authority; he was just a man doing a job, getting on with the business of making it in America.

"How you doing, Mr Prash?" the maintenance men would ask, keys jangling at their waists.

"Hanging in there!" Prash would answer, shaking a clenched fist for effect. Of all the new phrases he liked saying *Hanging in there!* It was what everyone said, and the words made him feel like a hardened survivor.

It was at this juncture, in this fluid swirling state of hardened wellbeing, that he became enmeshed with Leche.

Leche was a young Spanish-speaking girl who might have been considered a strange person though not in the category of strangeness Prash was hired to deter. Prash had noticed her from the beginning. She had a strange pattern of movements.

It gave him no reason to be suspicious at first. She left the building on her way to school (she was a high school senior, she'd tell him later). Within half an hour her mother – late for work, rummaging through her bag for a bus token, cigarette in her mouth – also left the building.

Minutes after her mother's departure Leche returned and marched back upstairs.

One morning he saw her waving at him through the glass door. She had apparently lost her keys. As he opened the door, he looked at her for the first time close up.

He saw the oval shape of her face, the pointed chin, the bleached whiteness of her skin; he saw eyes as round and sad as a doe's, and reddened from what he mistook for a school-girl's crying; he saw the gold bracelets, a button with a heart pinned on her coat, other trinkets that hinted at a schoolgirl's yearning for young womanhood.

Right at that moment she seemed so agitated, so distressed, he said to her with genuine concern, "You feeling all right?"

She looked at him as if she really wasn't all right, but it was none of anybody's business.

Later that same morning as he strolled down the stairs, stretching his legs, he glanced down the dimly-lit hallway of the second floor (not hers, she came down and went up with the elevator) and saw her again: leaning against a wall, one arm was folded over her belly; smoking with furtive urgency (Prash caught a whiff of what was undeniably marijuana).

He saw her long bare neck, her thin body stiff under the sweater and dress; he told himself, this high school senior not only cutting school, she doing other forbidden things; she's a real sharp girl.

This is when it started, baffling feelings, as strong as an ocean's undercurrent, pulling him down into the soul of this strange girl with her secret movements and habits: curiosity (why was she standing alone in an empty hallway, smoking? Outside whose door?), an itch to take advantage somehow of her secrets; a fatherly concern about her truancy; an older man's attraction to that thin resilient body she swung with such melancholy purpose through the door.

It should have been nothing more than an inflammation of his mind and loins, a harmless controllable flirtation.

But it was winter. There was now this dreary passage each day from one never-warm-enough interior to the next; this trudging along ice-slicked sidewalks, the wind slashing right to the balls of his eyes releasing tears; everything hard, confining and colourless.

And Prash was now a man of wings.

In Leche's frail body he saw the slender pliable promise of sugar-cane stalks; in her eyes the solitariness of the canefields and canals.

So that one morning as Leche was marching back in, confident she had duped her mother again, Prash said to her, out of pure whim, "I know you cutting school. I going to tell your mother."

She stopped; she looked at him; he laughed – *just a joke! your secret safe with me!* She walked away, then looked back at him, resentful, unsure. He smiled again – *I could keep secrets good!*

He kept his perch on a low limb of flirtation, fluttering his wings, following her with his eyes, hovering over her with his friendliness.

One afternoon she came up to him and said she needed four quarters, she had only a dollar note. Prash made a big show of reaching into his pockets and sorting out loose change. He refused to take her dollar note.

He teased her into revealing her secrets. She stood in the lobby, shifting from foot to foot, in turn shy and abrasive; and she told him that her father was a white man whom she'd never known; she had been conceived on the backseat of a Chevrolet car (she laughed at that last detail, though a taken-aback Prash couldn't see what was funny about it); school, she said, was boring; her life was boring; she longed to be out in the world, a working woman, her own apartment.

He rode the elevator with her – *I just taking a break!* – he wanted to know her name.

"Leche. That's Spanish for milk." She explained, "I liked drinking milk so much, I got stuck with the name." When she asked to borrow more money, he folded the note in the palm of her hand, squeezing it affectionately. On an impulse he followed this with a kiss on her cheek.

For several days after he did not see her. She didn't appear in the morning (leaving her bag near his desk, now that she'd won his trust). He wondered if she might be ill.

In the lobby people were constantly blowing their noses and sneezing as if near death and saying *Bless you!* He thought of taking the elevator up to her floor, knocking on the door to enquire. He wondered, again, if instead she'd rejected him as too old to be of any use; and with that thought came the realisation that his interest in this girl had grown into an unruly desire to know her intimately.

Why this desire for intimacy with a girl he barely knew, who lived with her mother and liked to drink milk? It never occurred to Prash to ask this question, to place his passion for Leche alongside his indifference (as Sookmoon still reminded him on occasion) to the fate of Moolchand and Ameena; alongside that brooding irritability breaking out like a rash on his body once he got back home and had taken off his jacket, his hat, his scarf, his gloves.

14. The Long Ride

His leg-stretching walks in the morning became more of a prowl along the floors (he sometimes startled old ladies in tattered cardigans with hair like white straw who didn't recognise him). He hung around the second floor, hoping to catch Leche once more in that furtive act of smoking marijuana.

He checked the numbers outside the doors on that floor, and compared these with names on the mailboxes.

One of the names was McBride. *Clyde 'The Slide'!*

It distressed him to think that Leche would have anything to do with someone like Clyde 'The Slide', whom he hadn't seen since that day in the lobby; who now struck Prash, because of this possible connection, as a slick, flashy worthless character, a dangerous competitor (younger and more moneyed) for her attention.

That side of him offering comfort and support now demanded that Leche make an appearance. He had to talk to her. He had to warn her about cultivating dangerous friendships, even if that meant getting involved in other people's affairs. Clyde 'The Slide' was the kind of character who wouldn't appreciate anyone *messing* (as he would put it) with his business; and Leche was volatile enough to tell Prash in a swift burst of anger to mind his own.

Days went by. Still no sign of her.

He went home, ate quietly, and spent restless nights playing out imaginary scenarios.

Sookmoon and Ameena were too busy clipping supermarket coupons, or flicking through mail order magazines to pay close attention to him.

Sookmoon had tried once to excite his interest with a recent purchase of Hallmark cards. With wondrous delight she had discovered that there was a card for every conceivable occasion

– from *Get Well* to *Condolences* – and for every relative one could possibly have. She had started mailing them off to people she knew back in the Republic. Prash, wrapped up in vigil and heated anxiety, refused to be drawn.

"What wrong with you, man? Why you so quiet?" Sookmoon probed.

Prash sucked his teeth and turned on his side in the bed.

"You hear the news 'bout Jaggernathsingh? His wife meet in accident and dead. Was in Canadian papers. A friend of mine send me the clipping. It happen three years ago and is only now the Canadian court order the people responsible to pay him damages. Some hundred thousand dollars in damages."

Silence. Prash's ears on fire. *Hundreds of thousands of dollars. To Jaggernathsingh.* His heart screaming in rage at how the wheels of justice turn in the world. Silence as heavy as a boulder in the bedroom to which he felt hopelessly strapped, and Sookmoon's words like so many sharp-beaked birds pecking at his chest.

"Moolchand thinking of moving back in," Sookmoon continued. "He living with one of these Spanish girls and her mother, but like they breaking up."

When even that revelation failed to move him in the obstreperous way she'd anticipated, she gave up. People have their moods, she told herself.

Actually, the last disclosure about Moolchand *living with one of these Spanish girls* distracted him for a while; it left him hungry for details and acidic with anger and envy; he started wondering what strategies his son had devised to get him that far, into the heart and into the bedroom of these women (*a Spanish girl and her mother!*); compared to Moolchand he, Prash, had gone only as far as offering money and unsolicited advice; and now he hadn't seen the girl in days!

Feeling more intensely alone, outclassed, overshadowed, rejected, he went back to creating scenarios of confrontation, big showdowns. Himself and Leche. Himself and Clyde 'The Slide'. Himself, Leche and Clyde 'The Slide'.

In almost all the scenarios he recognised himself emerging disgruntled, shame-faced, a loser.

His language still sounded borrowed, his accent uneven and brittle; he hadn't yet mastered those menacing gestures people made with their hands, even as they laughed. Leche seemed affronted by his concern and slapped him away easily with *fuckyous* and *shits*. Clyde 'The Slide' laughed at him, poked a finger in his chest, and sang life-snuffing refrains in his falsetto.

He had one violent dream in which he chased Clyde 'The Slide' up the stairs in a wild shoot-out, the bullets from Prash's gun going *ptweeng, ptweeng* in ricochet, for he was missing his target, until they got to the roof where a cornered Clyde stumbled back, back, back and fell over the side, right on the spot where the other security fellow had plunged to his death.

All this feverish imagining robbed him of sleep and diminished his appetite (Sookmoon had renewed her efforts to provide home-cooking). But Prash could not deny the excitement riding him each day he reported to his desk in the lobby, each day he waited. Such excitement had suffused his body once before, during those first days in America when he'd explored the streets, when he'd tested his bones and spirit against the elements, and tried out blue denims and hats before mirrors, wondering how he looked.

This situation, now in Prash's mind typically American in its dark possibilities, its potentially explosive character, left him with stark alternatives: he must do something about it or back away. If he backed away, dismissing the whole thing as foolish indulgence, he felt he would never win through when it

returned; he was certain it would return, with different players, but requiring similar bold moves on his part.

It was Ameena's sixteenth birthday. He was reminded of it
the night before by Sookmoon who spoke of its significance
(Sweet Sixteen) for American high school girls. He bumped into
Ameena coming out of the bedroom, her head bowed; he passed
her and said nothing.

The bathroom mirror was misty with steam from Ameena's
shower. He wiped it slowly with toilet tissue and for a long while
studied his face. The bathroom had been a source of early con-
tention, for Sookmoon insisted on decorating it (to Prash this
was a waste of money on so small a room); she also reminded
everyone of tiny rituals needed to keep it *looking nice*. It now
occurred to Prash that this highly furnished small room was
just right for his need to brood, his need for privacy.

That morning he stepped out of his building, the collar of
his jacket rolled up, and there to greet him was a sky as blue
and clear as any over the Republic. He hadn't seen a sky that
bright in a long time. In fact, when it wasn't obscured by tall
drab buildings or that wintry greyness, or by the need to con-
centrate on traffic lights and moving objects at his eye level,
the sky hardly existed.

For a while he felt embraced and energised by its light; but
there was the wind like a sharp clean blade slicing through his
body, bringing water to his eyes and spoiling any pleasure he
might have stirred up with thoughts of sunlit days back in the
Republic.

In the building lobby he fell to thinking about his taxi back
home and the condition of the unused battery (which he'd forgotten to remove).

He heard voices, high-pitched. He thought he recognised
one of them. He heard footsteps, a minor disturbance approaching.

Even before they appeared he knew it was Leche, and her mother, leaving the building together, for the first time, as if her mother had discovered her truant game – Prash couldn't tell from the rapid Spanish if that was the case – and was determined to put a stop to it.

He looked up momentarily, then pretended to be busy leafing through his newspaper. Leche's mother paused as was her habit to rummage through her handbag; Leche was about to push ahead through the door; then she too hesitated, waiting.

To Prash, mother and daughter might have chosen to stage this dramatic entry into the lobby: Leche pouting in muted rage, the mother reeling off her lines with a practised intensity. Prash looked up, first at Leche, her body rigid, her head disdainfully aiming for the freedom of the streets; she was dressed in shiny black boots, and though her face was a little blanched and thinner than when last he'd seen her, she looked glamorous in that dressy precocious way of high school girls.

He was hoping for a tiny gesture, a knowing glance his way. She appeared to be ignoring him.

He thought the framing of this scene in the lobby was perhaps a statement from her: *see how overbearing my mother can be? see what I have to put up with?*

When he looked at her mother – seeing her now as Leche's mother – he was struck, first, by her still youthful attractiveness; she was a short, feisty woman, with a pretty, chubby face (her daughter had no doubt inherited her tall skinny frame from the absent father) and though she wasn't evidently in competition with Leche, her body remained somehow firm and appealing. In fact, knowing what he knew about her, Prash felt at that moment a tender sympathy for her.

It was the first time he had felt drawn to a grown woman (Sookmoon, after all, would always be the young girl offered in marriage). He thought of her single-handed struggle to raise

Leche, to make amends for a stupid mistake that night in the backseat of the Chevrolet; he saw in her quick steps a wariness and distrust of all men; he sensed that raw tension, as of a leash held tight, between mother and daughter; and, not knowing why, he was drawn to the mother's side.

It was the more solitary side, the more violated side; and since Prash had been so often an instrument of violation back in the Republic, this might have been his first shiver of remorse.

In the next instant he said to the mother, "I know how you feeling. A pretty daughter can give a mother big headache."

Leche's mother looked at him, searching his face for what lay behind those words. Then she sighed, shook her head and said softly, with a grown woman's appreciation for the sentiment, "*Aie Dios!* ...Life is hell and then you die!"

Right at that point Prash felt shot at; he turned to Leche; her eyes burned into him from the door with a sharp pointed resentment, for he had taken the wrong side; he had, by inserting his concern at that moment, betrayed her.

Prash smiled, signalling his sworn loyalty; Leche snapped her head, having none of that!

And suddenly the scene was over, the players were moving on, and Prash was left to consider what he'd just witnessed.

His mind hovered, wings fluttering, over Leche's mother. How much at ease, how adult she had made him feel, not with her words, but with her eyes, in that single moment she'd searched his face. *Life is hell and then you die!* Spoken like someone who'd seen the grown man in his face, a man she thought she could, however briefly, share her troubles with. Never before had he felt touched or respected that way.

Spoken intimacies were not his style back in the Republic. Conversation in the rumshop, in his taxi, was a rancorous or boisterous thing; there you were with the boys; you spoke as man to man. And since he would always be older than Sook-moon, showing her a sensitive side was out of the question.

Something else, hardly before glimpsed, never before imagined, was suddenly possible with a woman; it had taken him all these years to catch a glimpse of that possibility here in this building lobby (he'd learnt to call it *a lobby* from Sookmoon) from a woman he hardly knew, whose daughter, he had to admit, he now wanted to know in his old hard cocksman way.

As other residents trooped out – the lobby in turn silent and echoing with morning chatter – Prash flew on a wing to a room upstairs where Leche's mother opened the door, smiled graciously and asked him in; where he sat sympathetic and absorbed as she spoke about her youthful mistakes (he would later tell her about his youthful excesses) slipping now and then into Spanish (apologising for that with girlish giggles) and waving her hands in that exciting Spanish way; where eventually she asked if Prash wanted a drink, or perhaps a cup of *Bustello* since he was still on the job.

Just as she got up to go to the kitchen, Prash was hailed by a loud voice in the lobby. *"My main man!* How you doing, my brother?" *Clyde 'The Slide'.*

Prash was jolted by his sudden appearance; it was all the more disturbing because Clyde 'The Slide' was wearing a three-piece suit under his coat and carrying a briefcase. He still walked like Henry Fonda but today he'd chosen a new cut and style to engage the world; his teeth were shiny, his face clean shaven, his falsetto exuberant.

Prash had come to the conclusion that, like those slick black fellows he'd noticed hanging around at street corners, Clyde 'The Slide' (who didn't leave the building on a nine to five job, and yet drove a fancy car) was a drug dealer. A drug lord. He had no real evidence of this apart from the gun in his waistband; Prash had never seen him dealing. It was nevertheless a very satisfying theory.

Now here he was attempting, it seemed, to impress Prash that he was a man of substance, stepping out on business that was nobody's business but which required formal dress.

Prash folded his arms, determined to look unimpressed, though he couldn't refuse slapping Clyde 'The Slide's' out-stretched palm the way the black fellows did.

"On my way out. Taking care of a little business," Clyde 'The Slide' said, carefully buttoning his coat (no pistol in his waistband this time). "Should be gone a couple of days. I know I can trust *my man here* to mind the store while I'm gone, right?" Palm outstretched again. "Take care, my man."

And Prash said, "Right."

And with that he was once more left alone at his desk, angry, churning, unhappy with himself.

But this was America! Life kept moving and changing all the time. The stage was empty one minute, then along came a cast of characters offering an entrance or exit, a chance to roll the dice and win: women and children who would be stars; chattering or strolling extras; *My main man!*

But wait! He too was a player! He could walk on any time and perform!

He could handle the best and the worst of human situations. Menace, sex, love, drugs, death on the roof – this was America! He could deal with it. Deal with it, walk away and live to tell the tale, tell many tales, in rumshops back in the Republic.

The appearance of the postman made Prash stop to consider that perhaps he was acting in a bizarre fashion, pacing the lobby and talking to himself. "How you doing?" Prash said brightly like a man who'd been caught zipping up his fly.

Of all the people coming and going the postman was the only white fellow Prash saw. He was as old as Prash (he let slip his age one day, lingering in the lobby, revealing somewhat brusquely that he was in the middle of divorce proceedings); his hair was thinning; he was not an unfriendly man; he went about his job with tight-lipped purpose, his finger flipping through the batch of envelopes, a smile, a few kind words to elderly women expecting social security cheques.

He said very little to Prash, apart from that single confessional lapse about his marriage, which Prash mistook for the beginning of a more open friendship. On his way out he might pause at the door to make a comment about the weather; Prash usually agreed with his comment; then he was gone.

Another player! Another possibility!

Serene life in a white neighbourhood somewhere beyond these fowlcoops of desperate living; a house with a lawn, near where the postman lived. He could handle that too!

It was time for his break, time to stretch his legs.

As he came down to the second floor, *something* told him he would find Leche there. She *was* there, her arm folded over her belly, the hallway smelling of marijuana. She saw him and smiled, as if something too had warned her he would appear. Their surprise and delight was electric.

"Wait, how you get back inside the building? You didn't pass through the lobby?" Prash said. Leche gave him a wicked grin and looked him boldly in the face, drawing him forward.

"You's a mysterious young lady," Prash said, shaking a reproving finger at her and laughing. And because she stood there, frail and alone, because she seemed happy to see him, he walked right up to her and kissed her on the cheek.

She threw her arms around his neck and held him in a long embrace. Prash allowed himself to be squeezed; under the sweater her body felt strange, wiry with a nervous energy; this was all new and startling to him, happening so quickly.

And because she wouldn't let him go, he pulled away from her and said, a little uneasy now, "You know you shouldn't be doing drugs." The light was dim in the hallway, but he could see her eyes reddened from all that marijuana.

"What should I be doing?" she asked, unnerving him again with her brash stare. Prash smiled, not sure how to continue. There was an awkward moment. She kissed him, in one frisky gambling movement.

"Want to try some?" she said, leaning back to the wall. She meant the marijuana. Prash put his hands in his pocket, uncertain.

"We can have fun together," she said. Prash put his fingers to his lips, telling her *Not so loud.*

"That's all right, we could do it in there," she said, pointing to the door behind Prash. *205/McBride.* Prash lost his smile.

"You don't have to worry. He's gone for the weekend," she said.

She produced a key and opened the door with such swiftness, Prash didn't have a moment to protest. He stood at the door, knowing he was about to cross into someone else's territory – *trespassing*, which is what those names and numbers on the doors hinted you would be doing if you weren't invited in.

She grabbed his hand and pulled him in.

McBride's territory. His apartment looked like a miniature palace furnished with a briefcase of money. The tables, the chairs, a chandelier, the curtains, the television set – everything seemed recently purchased. It made you stop, gasp and stare. Prash did just that. It made you wish you had the money to refurbish your own apartment. Sookmoon, Prash thought, would have wished exactly that.

How could McBride afford all this? Did he really *live* here? Did he really use every object in the apartment?

Prash, of course, had his theory, but before he could utter a word (and there was so much he wanted to say, questions he wanted to ask) Leche, who had disappeared in the kitchen, now came back, moving nimbly and familiarly across the carpeted floor.

"Close the fucking door!" she said. Her tone was sharp, like a whip cracking. She had this odd way of switching emotions, gentle and plaintive one moment, abruptly caustic the next. It baffled and annoyed Prash; he closed the door.

He stood dog-faced and frowning because he had just crossed borders of privacy, and he didn't like being snapped at by Leche, and he wasn't sure what would happen next. Leche waved her hands to the chairs, playful again, and invited him to make himself comfortable.

"I come here twice a week," she explained. "I get paid to clean the place. My mother doesn't know about this, *right?* She'd *kill* me if she found out."

Prash stood his ground, still puzzled, unsure. Leche came up to him, hooked her arms in his, and began a spontaneous tour of the apartment. "C'mon. You're so serious." she said.

Prash allowed himself to led from room to room; he relaxed, and feigned surprise or amazement as they poked their heads in every room. So many objects leapt to his eye inviting admiration or the mind's price tag; nothing looked worn by time or by overwashing; he tried to imagine what Leche did – dusting? washing dirty dishes? – when she cleaned the place.

At the door of McBride's bedroom she pranced inside and sat on the bed, looking at him with her sad doe's eyes. Prash ventured forward a few cautious steps, noticing the blue drapes, another television set, the half-closed door of a clothes closet through which he glimpsed shirts on hangers and a few ties.

"This is a water bed," Leche said, patting it, bouncing up and down. Prash nodded.

"*Mira*, I want to ask you a favour... I need money. I swear to God, I'll pay you back," she said, her tone now soft and urgent.

"You can ask me anything," Prash said, with a surge of confidence. "For you I'd conquer the whole world."

It was an old line he'd tried with dramatic success on young women in the Republic who knew only their drab villages and sang radio love songs and liked his sweetboy good looks and slicked combed-back hair.

Leche jumped off the bed, came up to him and kissed him again. "I like you," she said. "You're crazy sweet." She unbuttoned his jacket, she held him round the waist and squeezed him with her thin arms. "Crazy sweet!" she said.

My main man... crazy sweet.

"And for you, I'd do anything. I could *do* you now!" she said.

Her fingers fumbled with his belt; she knelt and unzipped his pants. Prash felt that stirring in his pants telling him his desire for sweetness had risen.

He looked around McBride's bedroom; he looked down at Leche's head; he felt her fingernails snagged in his hairs as she groped inside his shorts; when she put his swollen member in her mouth, he closed his eyes.

And he thought of evenings back in the Republic, sunset-tinged evenings in the backdam, where he had taken so many young girls, his knees chafing on cane trash; he thought of his adventures in rooms like cubicles with those city women who were businesslike and had skin like tough hide; he thought of Sookmoon, unspeaking, unmoving Sookmoon, who was finding all kinds of excuses these days for not doing it, who made no sound when she did it, who had this habit, the moment he had puffed and whimpered and expended himself, of nonchalantly scratching her thighs.

My main man... Crazy sweet!

A man could travel and conquer the whole world, and never know what it felt like to be taken this way. A man could climb mountains, speak volumes before adoring throngs, his hands lifted in blessing or triumph, and never know what it felt like to be *done* this way. After all these years, Prash thought (his fingers roaming her hair, his eyes still closed) after all these years driving his taxi, fleeing the Republic, he had discovered a new world of astonishing release, a prairie of the wildest pleasure.

He trembled as those years of hard tense living now drained out of him, *crazy sweet, man, crazy sweet*; he gripped Leche's shoulder with claws of the rawest need and for the first time in his life he screamed *Yes!* and *Oh gawd, girl!* to a woman, this skinny frightening Spanish-speaking American girl.

It was too much to bear. He opened his eyes, suffused with pleasure and gratitude; he pushed her gently away. She fell back on the water bed, her eyes wide and expectant, looking up at him. *Too much!*

"Hold on. I gotta go to the bathroom," he said.

He sat on the toilet seat – on a blue velour toilet cover, an item he had argued about bitterly with Sookmoon as unnecessary for *their* bathroom; his pants still unzipped, he was quivering with excitement, and a sudden creeping fear.

In his young days this would have been nothing, *nothing* at all. His only anxieties then, his only fear of catching anything, would have been from snakes wandering in the canefields, or a shot of syphilis from a city woman. Now here, in McBride's bathroom, he was gripped with apprehension.

To be caught on McBride's waterbed, his bottom exposed, to be caught in flagrant violation of some vague American law or right – this was now a strong possibility, with consequences too frightening to consider.

This girl could move fast!

Withdrawing to the bathroom was perhaps an indication he couldn't keep up with these young American girls. They moved too fast! Too fast!

He looked around McBride's bathroom; he saw a yellow toothbrush, floral shower curtains, pink hand towels; he saw a large red towel hanging on a rail. The bathroom looked just the way Sookmoon had tried to transform theirs despite his protests. Bathrooms were for washing; they were ordinary places for plain necessary functions – a shit, a shave and a shampoo. Why McBride would choose to decorate his bathroom this way – lace-trimmed blinds over the window, toilet bowl cover matching the colour of the rug! – was beyond Prash's understanding. To his theory about McBride he now added fresh doubts about the man's sexual preferences.

Leche was waiting for him outside on McBride's waterbed. Rising, Prash decided to wash his hands in the sink.

His movements were slow, deliberate, but it was as if calamity – unforeseen, volcanic – lay coiled inside the muscle of that moment, ready to explode.

He turned on the hot water tap, not too hard, he thought; the water gushed out with such force, it wet his trousers; in the sound of the spray he heard the doorbell ring. He shut off the tap and listened.

McBride? Returning so soon? He was supposed to be gone for the weekend!

He heard the patter of feet running to the door. That girl could move fast; she was smart; she could handle the situation. With his hand still frozen on the hot water tap, his heartbeat galloping, he listened.

He thought he heard voices; he strained to hear what was being said. Inside the bathroom he felt trapped; he'd have a lot of explaining to do unless Leche got rid of whoever was out there. That girl could handle the situation.

He listened. He waited.

The coil inside the muscle tightened again, a slow movement in the muscle of the moment.

Then there was a crashing sound, as if the ceiling had fallen in; another crashing sound, as from a gun, most certainly from a gun. His heart almost leapt out of his chest; a yelp of shock and fear escaped his lips; then silence, as the crashing sound vanished through the gaping holes it made in the air.

McBride! He hadn't gone anywhere. He had returned! McBride's gun – designed to take care of business! And the falsetto spiralling in outrage: *What the fuck you doing in my apartment?*

Crash. Darkness.

Prash waited for things to happen in just that sequence, fast and violent.

Nothing happened. No sound. No patter of returning feet; no knock on the bathroom door; no Leche laughing, assuring him, *It's all right.*

Oh gawd, girl! What trouble you get me in?

And the longer he waited, facing the door, half-expecting it to be kicked in, the more powerful was his sense of death trap; the more it seemed that darkness delayed was a mere turn of the door knob away; it was hanging about outside the door; it was letting him sweat some more; making him fall on his knees, tears streaming down his face; making him regret over and over his coming this country, his weakness for young girls, *all this foolishness, Oh gawd!*

He began to think of ways to elude the crashing darkness. There was a window in the bathroom. Perhaps if he opened it, he could climb out and escape; run like blazes down the backdam mud roads, past a boy whacking the rump of a cow he was driving home, deep into the canefields where he could hide; where neither McBride nor Leche nor anyone could follow him; and the pursuing darkness would be routed by the many ways of brighter sunlight.

He tried half-heartedly to open the bathroom window; it wouldn't budge; it seemed forever sealed; he remembered there was a long drop to the ground even though this was the second floor.

He backed away and was caught by his own face in the bathroom mirror; he froze; hair strands fell over his brow; his cheeks looked pudgy; it was his father's face; there were tears on his cheeks as thick as cane juice; he reached for the comb in his hip pocket.

He pushed his shirt in his pants, buckled up his belt, buttoned his jacket and, borrowing an expression he'd heard often on the streets, he said, "I'm outta here".

He didn't say it with the jocular disdain with which he had heard it used. The words were meant to quiet the drumming of his heart, to push him to the door.

He now believed that *something*, not just someone, lay waiting outside the door, wrapped in its silence, its horribleness; he had to confront it; walk out this tiny room and confront it.

"I'm outta here!" he said again. He turned the door knob and began singing, *Mahebuba O Mahebuba...*

The first thing he noticed as he stepped into the living room was the chandelier, still hanging, amazingly intact. He'd imagined it blown off the ceiling, its smashed pieces scattered everywhere on the carpet. Seeing it up there, glassy and glowing, gave him the briefest illusion that everything was all right. Indeed, nothing else look disturbed.

Out of the bathroom, through the living room, to the door – *outta here!*

He saw Leche; he saw her shiny black boots first, then he came upon her body, lying just as it had fallen on the waterbed, its arms and legs randomly spread, as if waiting for him to fall on top of her; only now she lay on the floor, her head turned limp to one side, as if she'd had no time to plead with the crashing darkness and had simply collapsed, her whole life sucked away through the holes in the air, leaving only bones and dry flesh under her clothes.

He stared at her face, white as snow, whiter than snow, drained of its life; her eyes were half-closed; her hair looked damp from the sweat of some astounding fear.

He leaned closer, searching for the tiniest shimmer of life; he reached down to touch the hair on her slender neck; the open mouth, that cavern of forbidden pleasure, sent a cold shudder through his body; once again he pulled back, not wanting to be sucked into that place of darkness, hoping she was really not dead, though she lay so completely still, limp and abandoned, so vacant of will.

Gulshanmen dil khilate hai.

Unbearable to stand there watching that face!

It was once part of his pleasure to watch the faces of young women contorted in pain, surprise, a stifled ecstasy; part of his pleasure as, with his back arched, he had brought them to a discovery of something beyond their narrow worlds, rooted in the here and now, in the *there* and *there* of his penetration. Leche's face, turned to one side in the same astonished way, holding him in a prolonged grinding stare, would not let him go. It made his lips move once more in song, in half-forgotten prayers.

With fingers that wanted to be certain, that still believed she was alive or asleep, he touched her chin; he moved her head; he saw the red pool of blood under the head, smearing her milk white face; the chin felt cold and heavy; the head in his fingers said no to his wailing plea to come back to life; said, Leave me alone, let me stay here in this red pool.

Unbearable, that white face, this chandeliered room!

He heard a sound at the door. His head snapped around; he saw the small face poked inside, watching him; he saw the boy's evil-relishing grin, the flash of silver braces; then it was gone.

That sound at the door gave him his release.

He almost shouted, *Come back here, you sonofabitch!* It would have done him no good.

Jaws had no discipline; he carried a gun, and listened to no one. Besides, what would he say to him? How would he explain his presence in McBride's apartment, standing over the body of a resident in the building?

Release: from a room in which he felt he'd been locked all his life. Release: by first resisting the impulse to call after Jaws (not knowing how long the boy had been standing at the door; not sure how much the boy had seen). Release: the click in his head (the lock finally picked, the vault door swinging open), and the realisation that this was all a frame-up.

There were always people *out there* trying to frameup your life.

Life in the Republic was a big frame; life anywhere was a frame; this situation in McBride's room – he could raise his hands and cry, *I had nothing to do with this; I don't know how I came here!* No one would listen.

The big frame! The body, the woman leading him on into that cavern of forbidden pleasure, the crashing darkness. *Big frame!*

The words, so right for this so typical American dilemma, came to him on a wing and hardened quickly into conviction. He liked its simple premise. It guaranteed release from rooms of unsatisfying living. It gave him what he needed instantly: a squirrel's chance of finding his way out.

"Fuck this shit!" Prash said.

The sound of those words, the powerful obscure magic of those words, made his stomach hard and unsparing. He started backing away from the body, looking around the room in case he'd forgotten something, the carpets mercifully hushing his retreat; reaching the door, turning, walking away – no problem, see? No problem.

"Fuck this shit!"

Down in the lobby he checked his watch; it was almost time to knock off; he put the visitors book away in the drawer of the desk for the guy on the next shift. He looked at his watch again; and he was ready to go.

He pushed through the glass door, rolled up the collar of his jacket; he braced himself for the first crisp challenge of wind, then he stepped forward into the cold sunshine.

Jab Saharamen milate hai, mai or tu...
Outta here!

15. HowYaDoing?

As she came off the plane she felt first the relief of being able to stretch her legs after an exhausting flight across oceans, which was how flights from New York to London always felt. Then a tingling excitement to be back home: the yellow cabs waiting outside, the streets and sidewalks of Manhattan, dense and strange and constantly streaming; and then her apartment, dropping her bag on the bedroom floor, making straight for the bathtub, an hour of wonderful warm sudsy soaking in the tub; telephone calls while she soaked; then her bathrobe, and catching up on her mail in bed.

Travelling gave her so much fine pleasure. The chance to dress up, the excitement of boarding aircraft, charming her way through customs and immigration; stepping out onto the streets of foreign capitals, duty-free shopping.

Here she was back at N.Y. Kennedy airport, which had a kind of tacky look these days: too many foreigners using it as a port of entry: those immigrants from the third world, clogging up the lines with bags and bundles of belongings, made it an undesirable place for business people, other travellers in suits, not sneakers and baseball caps, who these days prefer to enter the city through Newark, New Jersey.

At least this was what her companion was saying. Her companion and lover. She liked the idea of travelling abroad with her lover (she thought of him now as her lover, not her boyfriend, and no longer her "man".) This was the first time they had done it, flown off together, business and pleasure. All the romantic moments one could dream of were there: the furious couplings in strange bedrooms, the anonymity of hotels and cities. So many wild glamorous possibilities, so *do-able* once you'd got the time and the money.

But here she was walking toward the baggage claim centre, trying to remember where they said she could retrieve her bags; and wondering why her lover seemed so strangely distant, holding himself apart, or so she felt, once the plane had taken off for home.

And then an airport worker on one of those miniature airport courtesy carts drove by. A quick glance. She thought the face looked familiar. She kept walking. And then a voice behind her cried, "Champa?"

She didn't look around. She hadn't heard that name in quite a while. Even her companion had grown used to calling her Gail.

But then this courtesy car came rolling up beside her and the fellow at the wheel smiled as if he were driving a taxi and looking for a fare. And he said:

"Champa!... Wait, you don't know who this is?" She didn't know who it was, though the face looked familiar, and then, *Omigawd!* she knew who it was and she stopped walking.

The fellow smiling a big smile was her sister's husband. This was the last place she imagined meeting him again. If she kept walking he would follow her in this ridiculous courtesy car smiling and talking.

"What you doing here?" Prash asked, his face beaming with surprise and delight and a feverish anticipation of what he would tell Sookmoon when he got home.

"What are *you* doing here?" Champa shot back, as if the question was foolish and unnecessary.

"I working here now," Prash said, nodding his head, hoping she'd notice his service uniform, the short-sleeved white shirt with the airport personnel badge on the right shoulder, dark blue pants, black work boots, and of course the courtesy car he drove around.

"I working here," he repeated. There was an awkward silence. "So howyadoin', girl? Is a long time I ent see you. Like you travelling these days."

Then to demonstrate his familiarity with the airport procedures, Prash said, "Which plane you just come off... American 6565... or Continental 727?"

"I just came back from London" Champa said.

She had recovered from her initial embarrassment. She decided to talk to him as if he were an airport employee, not her sister's husband. "We're trying to find our bags."

The *we* slipped out. Prash looked at her companion. *So this was the black man Champa living with. Still living with after all these years.*

Prash nodded, touched his cap in a deferential salute, and said, "Howyadoing?" He was determined to be polite and friendly and, in that New York way, indifferent to what people did in their private lives.

"I think British Airways... Wait a minute," Prash looked thoughtful. "Yes, British Airways baggage centre is *waaay* 'cross there... on the concourse level... Look, allyou hop on, lemme drive you there."

Champa hesitated. She raised her hand, uncertain and un-willing.

"Is a long walk," Prash said. "I could get you there in a jiffy. This is my job. Helping passengers in situations like this. Hop on, man."

Champa looked at her companion. He seemed tired and noncommittal, and detached from her and this man who had called her Champa. They hopped on to Prash's motor cart and he drove off.

And now Champa resolved to fly from La Guardia or Newark airport next time. She wouldn't bump into her sister's husband there, have to suffer the indignity of riding on this stupid little vehicle, feeling helpless, looking ridiculous, which wouldn't have been her feelings had this happened at, say, Heathrow airport. And now he was striking up conversation as if she and her companion were a taxi fare he'd picked up in the streets.

"So how things, girl?" *Giurl!*

Champa decided not to say much, not to give the appear-ance of being too familiar with a worker – especially this talk-ing-so-loud worker! – at this tacky airport.

"How is Sookmoon?" she asked, stiff and grim-faced.

"She doing okay. You know she working with a family on Long Island... Yes, she left the Manhattan lady... Now she does take the Long Island Railway to get to work ...Yes, she doing okay."

"And the children?"

"The children doing okay... Ameena at college now."

Prash flashed her a look of pride as he turned a corner and came to a stop near an elevator. "She at St John's University.

Doing a degree in Business Administration. And she still have that job at the supermarket. Help pay her tuition."

The elevator door opened. Prash motored inside. The doors shut. Prash pressed the button for the concourse level.

Champa had never in her travelling life sat on a courtesy car in an elevator. She attempted to get off, but was restrained by Prash. She sat there feeling more ridiculous than ever.

On the concourse level Prash stepped on the gas as if to show his passengers what his motorised cart could do.

"The boy doing okay too. He working with Volvo Specialists."

"With whom?" Champa's companion suddenly spoke up.

"*Volvo Specialists*. They does fix only Volvo cars. As amarrafact, is he who fix the Volvo I driving. Bought it second hand, fix it up, now it running like new. *Mint condition!*"

"That's interesting. I must bring my Volvo to him for servicing."

"Anytime," Prash said, happy to show how broadminded and generous he could be; happy to discover there was some vital link, albeit a foreign motorcar, between his family and Champa's strange living arrangement.

He pulled up near the baggage carousel and was about to get off, offering now to help them secure the bags.

Champa firmly dissuaded him; she was effusive with thanks, playing to a knot of white people waiting for their bags, who weren't really paying as much attention to her as she imagined they were.

Prash kept chewing gum, smiling and nodding his pleasure at meeting her again so unexpectedly. He had put on weight; he seemed less boorish, less third-world hungry; more assured, with his new New York accent, his neat moustache, the flashy gold rings on his fingers. And Sookmoon, it seemed, was doing okay.

"You must drop in and see us," Prash said. "We living in Queens now."

Champa wished he would now simply go away.

"Tell Sookmoon to call me," she said, in a lowered voice, "and thanks for the help."

"You're very welcome!" Prash announced. He threw his miniature vehicle in gear and drove off with stylish arm motions.

And Champa was left to wait for her bags, standing beside her lover who quite suddenly put his arm around her shoulders; the gesture felt strange, perfunctory, as though he were making up for some perceived neglect. The man had definitely changed.

No longer her "man", he was something else, a creature given to strange bursts of tender affection, like this moment at the baggage carousel. That flowing feeling, that high voltage need of each other, the ocean-deep bond they had sustained over the years – was it her imagination or did it seem to be all of a sudden not there any more?

She wanted to get away quickly with her bags; she wanted to be back in her apartment; she longed to be in her hot tub, soaking and de-jetlagging, thinking about her wonderful trip to London and her lover; and now her sister Sookmoon and her husband: doing very well for themselves: coming to this country with half her possibilities and from all appearances making progress, making strides: catching up with her in that race across oceans: the pitter-patter of wandering hearts: the common pursuit of happiness.

OTHER TITLES BY N.D.WILLIAMS

THE CRYING OF RAINBIRDS

Torn between despair over 'the rancid taste of life on the island' and attachment to the 'irresistible, green island days', the characters in N.D.William's stories inhabit a Caribbean which is impossible to live in and impossible to live without. His characters dream of being whole and inviolable, but live in situations which are frequently on the edge of disorder and personal threat. Yet there is nothing wearily pessimistic about the tone of this collection. Williams's stories, like his characters, are intensely alive. Their individual voices button-hole us and won't let go. Their tales are often sad, but what passion they have in their pursuit of meaning!

"In Williams' brillaint final story... the urge to find release and return is given mystical and memorable expression..."

Chris Searle Liberation

ISBN 0948833 40 8 £4.95

THE SILENCE OF ISLANDS

"I came upon this tale of Delia one morning soon after she arrived. You could say it was thrust upon me under the most mysterious circumstances. A knock on the door and there she was, two bags at her feet like puppies of affection; a look on her face of disarray, as if she wasn't certain about what to say or do. And then this conversation.

    – Would you keep these bags for me, please. I have to go.

    – Yes, of course, but where are you going? I asked.

    – I must go now. Would you keep these bags?

    – Yes, yes, certainly, I said.

And she was gone."

In Delia Mohammed's bags, Mr. Ni Win finds a story of ascape from the suffocations of her father and Caribbean island life into the nightmarish world of an illegal alien in America.

He is moved by her refusal to be a victim and her determination to recreate herself in a hazardous and unfamiliar environment. Stalled in his own life, Mr. Ni Win is re-energised by reading Delia's account of her intense involvement with life and with literature.

"A terse and uncomfortable novel, which is executed with impressive detachment, reflecting the starving hearts of the exiles."

Chris Searle, *Morning Star*.

ISBN 0 948833 46 7

£6.95

THE VIEW FROM BELMONT
Kevyn Alan Arthur

The View from Belmont tells two stories: one through the letters of a young English widow who takes over her husband's cocoa estate in Trinidad in 1823; the other through the responses of a group of contemporary Trinidadians.

Clara's letters present the insights of a perceptive, independent-minded and generous-spirited young woman, who is nevertheless wholly committed to the institution of slavery. The letters give a sharp sense of the wider Trinidadian society, but at their heart is an account of Clara's relationships with those with whom she shares her life on the estate, particularly Kano, a 'loyal' slave whom she takes to her bed.

For the contemporary Trinidadians, the letters raise troubling questions about the nature of the national psyche, the absence of social consensus and the extent to which the history that the letters describe still shapes the present. This is a comic, painful and moving novel. Its presentation of the cruelties, violence and the casual affections of everyday relations under slavery raise questions not only about the nature of Caribbean societies, but the nature of history and its interpretation.

Kevyn Alan Arthur is the author of a poetry collection, *England and Nowhere*, published by Peepal Tree in 1992.

ISBN: 1-900715-02-3
Pages: 230pp
Price: £7.99 $14.00 US $17.50 CAN

The View from
BELMONT
Kevyn Alan Arthur

NOR THE BATTLE TO THE STRONG
Carl Jackson

From Imfe who is taken in slavery from Africa, Zero who is born a slave, Bam who lives to see emancipation, Tom who endures the long slow years of colonialism and Rocky who is active in the popular uprisings of the 1930s, *Nor the Battle to the Strong* is an unrivalled portrayal of the lives of five generations of an African Barbadian family. The careful research behind the novel gives the narrative rich and convincing texture, but it is the imaginative salvaging of the inner lives of this family which connects them to the present. Whilst frequently painful and disturbing, this is no recycled novel of abolitionist grievance, but an artistically shaped work of grief and hope. Jackson points to a longer historical context and a wider human truth in his reference to Ecclesiastes: 'The race is not to the swift, nor the battle to the strong, ... for time and chance happeneth to them all...'

This novel is part of an important return to historical subjects made by such contemporary Caribbean novelists as Caryl Phillips, David Dabydeen, Beryl Gilroy & Kevyn Arthur, and is an essential rewriting of the slavery narratives of earlier writers such as Edgar Mittelholzer. Whereas the latter co-opted the inhumanities of slavery to a pornography of violence, and restricted slave lives to the margins of his concerns, Jackson's treatment of the cruelties of the past is unflinching but controlled, and set within a larger context where the possibilities of redemption are never ruled out. Above all, he puts the historically voiceless at the articulate heart of his narrative.

Carl Jackson is the author of *East Wind in Paradise*, a political thriller published by New Beacon.

ISBN: 0-948833-97-1
Pages: 352pp
Price: £7.99 $14.00 US $17.50 CAN

UNCLE OBADIAH AND THE ALIEN
Geoffrey Philp

"If Dickens were reincarnated as a Jamaican Rastaman, he would write stories as hilarious and humane as these. Uncle Obadiah and the other stories collected here announce Geoffrey Philp as a direct descendent of Bob Marley: poet, philosophizer, spokesperson for our next new world."

Robert Antoni, author of *Blessed is the Fruit* and *Divina Trace*,
Winner of the 1992 Commonwealth Writers Prize.

Geoffrey Philp is a literary shaman, an enchanter, a weaver of spells that reveal unexpected and marvelous things about life, that carry the news of island culture to the mainland. From the first word of the first story in this comic and touching collection, Philp lifts me out of my world and drops me into the world of his charming, beleaguered and compelling characters. Uncle Obadiah and the Alien is one of those rare treasures, a book you can't put down and won't ever forget.

John Dufresne, author of *Louisiana Power & Light*

Geoffrey Philp's writing combines a poetic sensibility with finely honed narrative skills that draw on a multitude of resources: literary and oral traditions, rasta and ragamuffin flavours, science fiction and Jamaican tall tales. Philp blends them all with humour, wisdom and craft.

Norval Edwards

ISBN: 1-900715-01-5
Pages: 160pp
Price: £5.99 $10.50 US $13.00 CAN

SINGERMAN
Hazel D. Campbell

Realistic and magical, sombre and deeply comic, heroic and full of ironies, these stories explore the complexities of Caribbean reality through a variety of voices and forms.

In 'Jacob Bubbles', a short novella, Campbell connects the contemporary Jamaica of polical gang warfare to the past of slavery through the characters of Joseph, a runaway slave and his descendant, Jacob Bubbles, the fearsome leader of the Suckdust Posse. When Jacob Bubbles meets his death at the hands of Pantyhose, the female leader of a rival gang, a memory path opens in his head:

'to Papa Tee, a regular bullbucker and duppy conqueror chopping at human flesh; swearing at mothers with babies he had no intention of supporting; swearing in frustration in the line at the docks – no work this week, again! The blood leaking from him belonged to all of them – to Johnson, Papa Tee's father working the piece of land on the hillside which barely gave him enough to eat; to Cris-Cris, digging earth and coughing blood in a strange Spanish-speaking country; to Maas Sam, the obeah man at whom ghosts laughed; to William, chased off the estate because he asked for more wages; to all of them passing swiftly back into time; back to Jacob, the runaway slave pausing under a tree to rearrange his human burdens so that he could make a faster escape into the forest, up into the mountains to freedom.'

In these stories there is an acute perception of the ways in which poverty, racism and sexism can maim the spirit. But if there is one overarching vision, it is of the redemptive power of hope and love and the people's capacity to rise out of enslavements old and new.

ISBN: 0-948833-44-0
Pages: 155pp
Price: £4.95 $9.50 US $11.00 CAN